A sha... the sa... woman with big, dark eyes stared out at Ariel.

David took Ariel's hand. "Let's go see if anyone's home," he said, looking straight at the house, at the woman on the porch. But he didn't see her. Ariel realised she wasn't real. Not any more.

"N...s?" David asked. "Don't worry, Ariel. ...I'm with you."

...someone else...in spirit. Was the ...too? She didn't have to wait long ... As they walked across the porch, ...door creaked open. Even in the dim ...lighting, Ariel glimpsed the dangling

...od!" David rushed forward, but Ariel ...arm, her fingers clutching at his

...o late." Even without seeing the ...blank stare from a stiff face drained of ... Ariel would have known she was already ...er ghost hovered near her body, her ... as she tried to communicate.

"A... you all right?" David said.

"I'... But she had a feeling she might not ...g. As David had warned earlier, this ...urned out to be a dead end. For this poor ...man.

And for Ariel.

Dear Reader,

I'm thrilled to be writing for Mills & Boon's new paranormal line, Nocturne. My fascination with the supernatural began on my birthday one dark, stormy night, when, if my brother Tony is to be believed, a witch left me on our parents' doorstep. While my only special ability is an overactive imagination, the heroines in my three-book series for the Intrigue Nocturne line have far more compelling gifts.

In *Haunted*, Ariel Cooper can see the ghosts of those who have recently died. She considers her ability a curse because it has only brought her pain and rejection. But when someone begins a witch hunt, killing off her relatives, Ariel has to accept and utilise her ability to save herself and the man she loves. Unlike Ariel, I don't consider my gift a curse, not even when I can't sleep at night for coming up with new plots and scenes. I hope you enjoy *Haunted*!

Thanks!

Lisa Childs

Look for *Persecuted* in September 2008 – the witch hunt continues!

Haunted
LISA CHILDS

MILLS & BOON®
Pure reading pleasure™

*First published in Great Britain 2008
by Harlequin Mills & Boon Limited,
Eton House, 18-24 Paradise Road, Richmond, Surrey TW9 1SR*

© Lisa Childs-Theeuwes 2006

ISBN: 978 0 263 85982 9

46-0808

*Harlequin Mills & Boon policy is to use papers that are
natural, renewable and recyclable products and made from
wood grown in sustainable forests. The logging and
manufacturing processes conform to the legal environmental
regulations of the country of origin.*

*Printed and bound in Spain
by Litografia Rosés S.A., Barcelona*

ABOUT THE AUTHOR

Award-winning author Lisa Childs wrote her first book when she was six, a biography of the family dog. Now she writes romantic suspense, paranormal romance and women's fiction. The youngest of seven siblings, she holds family very dear in real life and her fiction, often infusing her books with compelling family dynamics. She lives in west Michigan with her husband, two daughters and a twenty-pound Siamese cat. For the latest on Lisa's spine-tingling suspense and heartwarming women's fiction, check out her website at www.lisachilds.com. She loves hearing from readers who can also reach her at PO Box 139, Marne, MI 49435, USA.

To Tara Gavin, Jennifer Green and Jenny Bent
– working with such awesome, inspiring ladies
has been a wonderful gift!

To Paul, Ashley and Chloe – my family –
the greatest blessing in my life!

Prologue

Europe, 1655

Strong hands closed over her shoulders, shaking her awake. Elena Durikken blinked her eyes open, but the darkness remained, thick, impenetrable.

"Child, awaken. Quickly."

"Mama?" She blinked again, bringing a shadow into focus. A shadow with long, curly hair. "Mama."

"Rise up. Hurry. You have to go." Her mother's strong hands dragged back the blankets, letting the cold air steal across Elena's skin.

"Go? Where are we going?" She couldn't remember being awake in such blackness before. Usually a fire glowed in the hearth, the dying embers casting a glow over their small home. Or her mother burned candles, chanting to herself as she fixed her potions from the dried herbs and flowers strung from the rafters.

"Only you, child. You must go alone." Mama's words, the final way she spoke, chilled Elena more than the cold night air.

"Mama…" Tears burned her eyes and ran down her face.

"There's no time. They will come soon. For me. And if you are still here, they will take you, too."

"Mama, you are scaring me." It was not the first time. She had scared Elena many times before, with the things she saw, the things she *knew* were coming before they ever happened.

Like the fire.

"Is this…is this because of the fire, Mama?"

Mama didn't answer, just pulled a cape over Elena's head, lifting the hood over her hair. Then she slid Elena's feet into her boots, lacing them up as if she were a small, dependent child, not a thirteen-year-old girl she was sending alone into the night. Mama pressed the neck of a satchel against Elena's palm. "Ration the food and water. Keep to the woods, child. Run. Keep running…."

"How can they blame you for the fire?" she cried. "You warned them."

Even before the sky had darkened or the wind had picked up, her mother had told them the storm was coming. That the lightning would strike in the night, while the women slept. And that they would die in a horrible fire. Mama had seen it all happen....

Elena didn't know how her mother's visions worked, but she knew that Mama was always right. More tears fell from her eyes. "You asked them to leave."

But the woman of the house, along with her sister-in-law whose family was staying with her, had thought that with their men away for work, that Mama was tricking them. That she, a desperate woman raising a child alone, would rob their deserted house. She'd been trying to save their lives.

Mama shook her head, her hair swirling around her shoulders. "The villagers think I cast a spell. That I brought the lightning."

Elena heard the frightened murmurs and saw the downward glances as her mother walked through the village. Everyone thought her a witch because of the potions she made. But when the townspeople were sick, they came to Mama for help even though they feared her. How could they think she would do them harm? "No, Mama..."

"No. The only spell cast is upon me, child. These visions I see, I have no control over them," she said. "And I have no control over what will happen now. I need you to go. To run. And keep running, Elena. Never stop. Or they will catch you."

Elena threw her arms around her mother's neck, more scared than she had ever been. Even though she heard no one, saw no light in the blackness outside her window, she knew her mama was right. They were coming for her. The men who'd returned, who'd found their wives, sisters and daughters dead, burned.

"Come with me, Mama," Elena beseeched her, holding tight.

"No, child. 'Tis too late for me to fight my fate, but you can. You can run." She closed her arms around Elena, clutching her tight for just a moment before thrusting her away. "Now run!"

Tears blinded Elena as much as the darkness. She'd just turned toward the ladder leading down from the loft when Mama caught her hand, squeezing Elena's fingers around the soft velvet satchel. "Do not lose the charms."

Elena's heart contracted. "You gave me the charms?"

"They will keep you safe."

"How?" Elena asked in a breathless whisper.

"They hold great power, child."

"You need them." Elena did not know from where they had come, but Mama had never removed the three charms from the leather thong tied around her wrist. Until now.

Mama shook her head. "I cannot keep them. They are yours, to pass to your children. To remember who and what we are."

Witches.

Mama did not say it, but Elena knew. She shivered.

"Go now, child," Mama urged. "Go before it is too late for us both." She expelled a ragged breath of air, then pleaded, "Do not forget...."

Elena threw her arms around her mother's neck, pressing her face tight against her, breathing in the scent of lavender and sandalwood incense. The paradox that was her mama, the scent by which she would always remember her. "I will never forget. Never!"

"I know, child. You have it, too. The curse. The gift. Whatever it be."

"No, Mama..." She didn't want to be what her mother was; she didn't want to be a witch.

"You have it, too," Mama insisted. "I see the power you have, much stronger than any of mine. *He* would see it, as well, and want to destroy you." Before Elena could ask of whom her mother spoke, the woman pushed her away, her voice quavering with urgency as she shouted, "You have to go!"

Elena fumbled with the satchel as she scrambled down the ladder, running as much from her mother's words as her warning. She didn't want the curse, whatever the mystical power was. She didn't want to flee, either. But her mama's fear stole into her heart, clutching at it, forcing her to run.

Keep to the woods.

She did, cringing as twigs and underbrush snapped beneath the worn soles of her old boots. She had run for so long her lungs burned and sweat dried on her skin, both heating and chilling her. She'd gone a long way before turning and looking back toward her house.

She knew she'd gone too far, too deep into the woods to see it clearly with her eyes. So, like Mama, she must have seen it with her mind. The fire.

Burning.

The woman in the middle of it, screaming, crying out for God to forgive them. Pain tore at Elena, burning, crippling. She dropped to her knees, clutching her arms around her middle, trying to hold in the agony. Trying to shut out the image in her head. She crouched there for a long while, her mama's screams ringing in her ears.

Run, child. Her mother's words sounded in her head. *Keep running.*

She forced herself up, staggering on her weakened legs, turning away from all that she'd known, all that she'd loved.

Behind her, brush rustled, the blackness shattered by the glow of a lantern. Oh, God, they'd found her already.

The glow fell across her face and that of the boy who held the lantern. Thomas McGregor. He wasn't much older than she, but he'd gone to work with his father and uncles, leaving his mother, sister, aunt and cousins behind…to burn alive.

As they'd burned her mother. "No…"

"I was sent to find you. To bring you back," he said, his voice choked as tears ran down his face. Tears for his family or for her?

Her mother had seen this, had tried to fight this fate for her daughter, the same fate that had just taken her life.

"You hate me?" she asked.

He shook his head, and something flickered in his eyes with the lantern light. Something she had seen before when she'd caught him staring at her. "No, Elena."

"But you wish me harm? I had nothing to do with your loss." Nor did her mother, but they had killed her. Smoke swept into the woods, too far from the fire to be real, and in the middle of the haze hovered a woman. Elena's mother.

"I have to bring you back," Thomas said, his hand trembling as he reached for her, his fingers closing over her arm.

The charms will keep you safe.

Had her mother's ghost spoken or was it only Elena's memory? Regardless, she reached in the pocket of her cape, clutching the satchel tight. Heat emanated through the thick velvet, warming her palm. As if she'd stepped into Thomas's mind, she read his thoughts and saw the daydreams he had had of the two of them. "Thomas, you do not wish me harm."

"But Papa…"

Other memories played through Elena's mind, her mother's memories. She shuddered, reeling under the impact of knowledge she was too young to understand. "Your papa is a bad man," she whispered. "Come with me, Thomas. We will run together."

He shook his head. "He would find us. He would kill us both."

Because of what she'd seen, she knew he spoke the truth. Eli McGregor would kill anyone who got between him and what he wanted.

"Thomas, please…"

His fingers tightened on her arm as if he were

about to drag her off. Elena clutched the satchel so closely, the jagged little metal pieces cut her palm through the velvet.

He shuddered as if a great battle waged inside of him. "I cannot give you to him. Go, Elena. You are lost to me." But when she turned to leave, he caught her hand as her mother had, trembling as he pressed something against her bloody palm. "Take my mother's locket."

To remember him? To remember what his family had done to hers? She would want no reminders. But her fingers closed over the metal, warm from the heat of his skin. She couldn't refuse. Not when he had spared her life.

"Use it for barter, if need be, to get as far away from here as you can. My father has sworn vengeance on all your mother's relatives and descendents. He says he will let no witch live."

"I am not a witch." She whispered the lie, closing her eyes to the glowing image of her mother's ghost.

"He will kill you," Thomas whispered back.

She knew he spoke the truth. Like her mother, she could now see her fate. But unlike her mother, she wouldn't wait for Eli McGregor to come for her. She turned to leave again, then twirled back, moved closer to Thomas and pressed her lips against his cheek, cold and wet from his tears.

"Godspeed, Elena," he said as she stepped out of the circle of light from his lantern, shifting into the darkness and the smoke, letting it swallow her as she ran.

This time she wouldn't stop…she wouldn't stop until she'd gotten as far away as she could. And even then, she wouldn't ever stop running….

From who and what she was.

Armaya, Michigan, 1986

The candlelight flickered as the wind danced through the open windows of the camper, carrying with it the scent of lavender and sandalwood incense. Myra Cooper dragged in the first breath she'd taken since she'd begun telling her family's legend; it caught in her lungs, burning, as she studied her daughters' beautiful faces.

Irina snuggled between her bigger sisters, her big, dark eyes luminous in the candlelight. She *heard* everything but, at four, was too young to understand.

Elena, named for that long ago ancestor, tightened her arm protectively around her sister's narrow shoulders. Her hair was pale and straight, a contrast to Myra and Irina's dark curls. Her eyes were a vivid icy blue that *saw* everything. But, at twelve, she was too old to believe.

Ariel kept an arm around her sister, too, while her gaze was intent on Myra's face as she waited for more of the story. The candlelight reflected in her auburn hair like flames, and her green eyes glowed. She listened. But Myra worried that she did not hear.

She worried that none of them understood that they were gifted with special abilities. The girls had never spoken of them to her or one another, but maybe that was better. Maybe they would be safer if they denied their heritage. Yet they couldn't deny what they didn't know; that was why she had shared the legend. She wanted them to know their fate so they could run from it before they were destroyed.

"We are Durikken women," she told her daughters, "like that first Elena."

"You named me after her," her oldest spoke, not questioning. She already knew.

Myra nodded. "And I'm named for her mother." And sometimes, when she believed in reincarnation, she was sure she was that woman, with her memories as well as her special abilities.

However, most of the time Myra believed in nothing; it hurt too much to accept *her* reality. But tonight she had to be responsible. She had one last chance to protect her children; she'd already failed them in so many ways. They didn't have to live the hardscrabble life she'd lived. They didn't have to be what she was—a woman whose fears had driven her to desperation.

"Our last name is Cooper," Elena reminded her.

"Papa's name," she said, referring to her own father. None of their fathers had given his child his name, either because the man had refused or she hadn't told him he was a father. "We are Durikken, and Durikken women are special. They know things are going to happen before they happen."

Pain lanced through Myra, stealing her breath again as images rolled through her mind like a black-and-white movie. She couldn't keep running and she couldn't make *them* keep running, either.

She forced herself to continue. "They see things or people that no one else can see. This ability, like the charms on my bracelet—" she raised her arm, the silver jewelry absorbing the firelight as it dangled from her wrist "—has been passed from generation to generation."

But Myra was more powerful than her sisters, had inherited more abilities as a woman and a witch. That was why she had been given the bracelet— because her mother had known she would be the only one of her three daughters to continue the Durikken legacy.

Myra's fingers trembled as she unclasped the bracelet. She'd never taken it off, not once since her mother had put it on her wrist, until tonight. Her daughters had admired it many times, running their fingers over the crude pewter charms, and she knew which was each one's favorite.

Elena had always admired the star, the sharp tips now dulled with age. Irina loved the crescent moon, easily transformed—like Irina's moods—from a smile to a frown, depending on the angle from which it dangled. Ariel favored the sun, its rays circling a small, smooth disk. Despite its age, this charm seemed to shine brighter than the others. Like Ariel.

Even now, in the dingy little camper, an aura surrounded the child, glowing around her head as spirits hovered close. Did Ariel know what her gift was? Did either of her sisters? Her daughters needed Myra's guidance so they could understand and use their abilities. They were too young to be without their mother, but she couldn't put them at risk. All Myra could hope was that the charms would keep them safe, as they had that first Elena so long ago.

Myra knelt before her children where they huddled in their little makeshift bed in the back of the pickup camper, their home for their sporadic travels. This was all she'd been able to give them. Until now. Until she'd shared the legend.

Now she'd given them their heritage, and with the help of the charms, they would remember it always. No matter how much time passed. No matter how much they might want to forget it or ignore it. Like that Elena from so long ago, even though she'd feared her future and tried to outrun it, she'd never thrown away the charms. She'd known how important they were, and so would Myra's children.

She reached for Elena's hand first. It was nearly as big as hers, strong and capable, like the girl. She could handle anything...Myra hoped. She dropped the star into Elena's palm and closed her fingers over the pewter charm. The girl's blue gaze caught hers, held. No questions filled her eyes, only knowledge. At twelve, she'd already *seen* too much in visions like her mother's. The girl had never admitted it, but Myra knew.

She then reached for the smallest—and weakest—hand, Irina's. Myra worried most about this child. She'd had so little time with her. She closed Irina's hand around the moon. *Hang on tight, child.* She didn't say it aloud; for Irina, she didn't need to—the child could hear unspoken thoughts.

Myra swallowed down a sob before reaching for Ariel. But the girl's hand was outstretched already. She was open and trusting, and because of that might be hurt the worst.

"Don't lose these," she beseeched them. Without the protection of the little pewter charms, none of them would be strong enough to survive.

"We won't, Mama," Elena answered for herself and her younger sisters as she attached her charm to her bracelet and helped Irina with hers.

Despite her trembling fingers, Myra secured the sun charm on Ariel's bracelet, but when she pulled back, the girl caught her hand. "Mama?"

"Yes, child?"

"You called it a curse…this special ability," Ariel reminded her, her voice tremulous. She had been listening.

Myra nodded. "Yes, it is a curse, my sweetheart. People don't understand. They thought our ancestors were witches who cast evil spells."

And they had been witches, but ones who'd tried to help and heal. Her family had never been about evil; that was what had pursued them and persecuted them throughout the ages.

"But that was long ago," Elena said, ever practical. "People don't believe in witches anymore."

Myra knew it was better to warn them, to make them aware of the dangers. She'd shown them the locket earlier, the one nestled between her breasts, the metal cold against her skin. It was the one Thomas had pressed upon Elena all those years ago. Inside were faded pictures, drawn by Thomas's young hand, of his sisters, who had died in the fire. Their deaths could have been prevented if only they'd listened and fought their fate. "Some still believe."

"Mama, I'm cursed?" Ariel asked, her turquoise eyes wide with fear. Her hand trembled as she clutched the sun.

No one more than I. Myra had lost so much in her life. Her one great love—Elena's father. And now...

"Mama, there are lights coming across the field!" Ariel whispered, as if thinking that if she spoke softly they wouldn't find her. Maybe she didn't hear as much as her sisters, but she understood.

Myra didn't glance out the window. She'd already seen the lights coming, in a vision, and so she'd hidden the camper in the middle of a cornfield. But still they'd found her; they'd found *them.* She stared at her children, memorizing their faces, praying for their futures. Each would know a great love as she had and all she could hope was that theirs lasted. That they fought against their fate, against the evil stalking them, as she would have fought had she been stronger.

She just stood there next to the camper, in the middle of the cornfield, as they took her children away. The girls screamed and reached for her, tears cascading down their beautiful faces like rain against windows.

This wasn't Myra's final fate; her death would come much later. But as her heart bled and her soul withered, this was the night she really died. The night her children were taken away.

Chapter 1

The wailing sirens and shouting voices receded to a faint hum as the light flashed before Ariel's eyes. Glowing through a thin veil of mist, bright but not blinding, it granted her such clarity that she could see what others could not.

The little girl. Her big, dark eyes wide in her pale face, her black hair hanging in limp curls around her cheeks and over her shoulders. In that pale yellow dress she'd favored, she was dressed for school. But she wasn't there, safe in Ariel's second-grade classroom. Not now. She hovered before the ramshackle house, back from the curb where police cars and an ambulance blocked the street.

Ariel had left her Jeep farther down the road and walked to the house, which sat on the edge of commercial property, only businesses and warehouses surrounding it and a handful of other rundown rental houses. No trees. No grass. No yard in which a child could play. Ariel had ducked under the crime scene tape roping off the property. She didn't need to rush around like all the other people, the ones trying to figure out what had happened or how to help. Before she'd even arrived, she'd known what had happened and that it was too late for help.

As she blinked back tears, the mist thickened and the light faded, dimly shining on just the little girl, who, too, was fading and dissolving into the mist. Ariel reached out a hand, trying to hold on to her, trying to keep her from leaving. Her voice thick with emotion, she whispered the child's name, "Haylee…"

The little girl whispered back, her mouth moving with words Ariel couldn't hear. What did she want to tell her? Goodbye?

The tears fell now, sliding down Ariel's cheeks, blurring Haylee from her vision. "I'm not ready to let you go…."

She was too young to be alone. Only eight. And she'd get no older now.

Ariel's heart ached so much she trembled with the pain. As she shook, the charm dangling from the bracelet on her wrist swayed back and forth. Her hand was still extended, reaching for Haylee as the child faded away. Ariel's fingers clutched at the mist, slipping through the gossamer wisps until she touched something solid. Something strong and warm.

Arms closed around her. A hand pressed her face against a hard shoulder. On a gasping breath, she drew in the rich scent of leather and man. *Her man.*

Even with her eyes closed, she saw David as vividly as if she were staring up at him. Although she wasn't petite at five ten, David towered above her and everyone else. With his golden hair and dark eyes, he was a throwback to the conquering Vikings of centuries ago, not so much in appearance as attitude. Or perhaps a black knight, for he was dressed all in black today—black leather jacket, black silk shirt and black pants.

His deep voice rumbled as he told her, "You shouldn't be here. I'm going to take you home."

"H-how did you know?" she asked. How did he always know where she was and when she needed him? She hadn't called him. She should have. She realized that as she glanced up at his face, his square jaw taut and hard, his dark eyes guarded. But she'd called Ty McIntyre instead—for his badge, not his support.

"Did Ty call you?" Of course the police officer would have called David. They'd been best friends since they were little kids—or so they'd told her. She hadn't known either man that long, just long enough to fall for David.

"Ty's here?" David asked. "Oh, my God, is he the injured officer?"

Ariel blinked the last of the mist away. As it vanished, the faint hum she heard morphed into a cacophony of sirens and shouts. For the first time since arriving on the scene, she became aware of the reporters shouting out questions from the curb as officers held them back. "Mr. Koster, why are you here? What's your involvement?"

Her. If Ty hadn't called David, the live coverage of the scene must have been how he'd known where she was. She didn't ask him, though, because he'd started toward the house. Unlike the media, the officers never attempted to stop him. Everyone knew the richest man in Barrett, Michigan.

They didn't know her. Until David's appearance, neither the police nor the reporters had really noticed her.

"Who is that with you?" a reporter called out

now as Ariel followed David, his shadow falling across her.

"Who's the redhead?" another one shouted.

David ignored them, intent on the house, its door gaping open on broken hinges.

"Ty's hurt?" she asked him, her voice cracking. She never would have called him had she known it would put him in danger.

"I don't know. I have to find him," David said, then glanced down at her. "But I don't want you to come inside the house."

His dark eyes soft with concern, he obviously feared what she might see. If he only knew… But that was perhaps the only thing he didn't know about her—what she saw. She couldn't tell him because she couldn't explain what she didn't understand herself.

"I'll be all right," she promised him. It was an empty promise because she had no way of knowing if she spoke the truth. No way of knowing what might happen next. That gift had been her mother's, not hers.

He must have assumed she meant she'd be okay by herself outside, for he withdrew his arm and started toward the gaping door. But before he could step inside, two men filed out wearing medical examiner's jackets and carrying a small black body bag on a gurney between them.

Haylee's body, battered and broken, lay inside that bag. But not her spirit. Her spirit hovered yet on the mist, which thickened even as the light brightened. Everything receded again, the shouts of the reporters, the flashes of their cameras. She saw nothing but Haylee again.

"Ariel." David called her name as his arm came around her shoulders, lending his strength and support with his closeness.

"Where's Ty?" she asked, but a glance up answered her question. The officer stood near David, his dark hair rumpled, his face swollen and blood seeping through his dark T-shirt.

"What the hell happened?" David asked his friend.

Ty blew out a ragged breath. "Son of a bitch killed his daughter, then resisted arrest."

"Wh-where is he?" Ariel stammered.

He nodded toward the house. "Still inside."

"He's dead?" David asked.

Another nod.

Ariel hadn't *seen* Haylee's father. But then, since he'd abused his own child, he'd probably lost his soul long ago. She gestured toward Ty's T-shirt, where the blood seeped. "You're hurt. You need help."

With just a look toward the curb, David summoned paramedics, who rushed up to help his friend. "Take him to Mercy," he directed them. "Dr.

Meadows will be waiting." His cell phone was out, pressed to his ear, before Ty could be helped toward the ambulance.

He refused the gurney, walking by himself instead. As he moved forward, unbeknownst to him, he stepped into the mist and passed through the fading image of Haylee. Ariel gasped as he turned back, his blue gaze meeting hers for just a moment before he swayed on his feet.

"He'll be all right," David said, his voice even deeper with conviction. "He's strong."

Despite his claim, David led her back toward the ambulance into which Ty was being helped. All color had drained from the officer's face, leaving it as stark and pale as Haylee's. He whispered to Ariel, too, but his words she heard. "I'm sorry."

She shook her head, the regret all hers. She hadn't sent him here to help Haylee. She'd known it was already too late for that when the mist had swirled into the classroom where she taught second grade and the student she'd thought absent had appeared. Like so many others Ariel had seen over the years—as a ghost.

The woman reached trembling fingers toward the television, brushing them over the image on the screen. Although the glass was cold beneath her skin, warmth spread through her. "Ariel…"

Not much of the child she'd been was left in the beautiful woman Ariel had become. Her hair was long now and a richer, more vibrant red that stood out like blood against the dead lawn of the property surrounded by crime-scene tape. Her face had thinned, her eyes, large and haunted, overpowering the delicate features of her nose and mouth.

Haunted. That was what this child was. The camera caught her reaching out toward empty space, but Myra knew what her daughter saw. The spirits had always been drawn to Ariel, even when she'd been a child. Myra wasn't sure if Ariel had seen them then, but she obviously saw them now.

Then Myra glimpsed the charm dangling from Ariel's thin wrist. She slid her fingertips across its image on the screen. Even though she touched glass, not the charm, she felt the heat of the little pewter sun, power radiating from it. If Ariel only knew…

Myra should have told her children everything that night so long ago when they'd been taken from her. She should have prepared them better to deal with their gifts and the curse. But they'd been so young.

Tears burned her eyes, blinding her to Ariel's face. Giving them up had been the hardest thing she'd ever done, but they'd deserved better than her. They had deserved to live as normal lives as they could with the gifts they'd inherited. They'd deserved to be safe.

Pain pounded at her temples as pictures rolled through Myra's mind, visions of her children. They weren't safe. Not anymore. Maybe she'd given them up for nothing. She hadn't hidden them from danger; she'd made them more vulnerable to it.

Weak in the knees, Myra settled back onto the hard wooden chair next to the round table covered with a brightly patterned cloth like the ones covering the walls that transformed her little trailer from drab to exotic. In the middle of the table a crystal ball glittered, reflecting the images from the television.

Mostly she used the ball as a prop, something to open the wallets of superstitious souls looking for a brighter future. So she didn't always tell them what she saw inside her head but what she knew they wanted to hear. For a little while, they'd be happy and she'd be richer. But just for a little while.

That was as long as her happiness had ever lasted, when she'd fallen for Elena's dad, when she'd had her children. She'd never been able to keep anyone she'd loved. She'd like to blame the curse, but she suspected it was her own fault, her cowardice.

But could anyone be happy forever? She would never know.

She leaned over the table, peering into the

crystal. Myra could see no future in that ball, not for her. Not for her children.

All that reflected in the crystal was the television screen, the flash of red of Ariel's long hair, startling against the cream-colored sweater she wore. Myra lifted her gaze to the TV, to the face of her beautiful daughter. The camera zoomed in, catching the anguish brightening her turquoise eyes with unshed tears.

"Oh, baby, it might already be too late for you," she said on a ragged sigh. "Like it's too late for me."

She didn't have time to warn them; if she tried, she might lead the threat to their doors. She didn't have time to run. She'd seen the danger and it was closing in on her. Fast. It might already be stalking her children.

"Keep your eyes open, baby," she advised her daughter, wishing Ariel could hear her. But telepathy wasn't this child's gift.

"He might already be there, with you," she warned as a man's arms closed around the woman on television, pulling her close. To protect her? Or harm her?

Hopefully her daughter had better taste in men than she had. Myra had chosen the wrong man to love, one who would never be able to love her back. But then, no man had been able to do that…once they'd learned the truth about her. That was why she'd started using them: for money, for security.

But even that hadn't lasted. They'd paid her to go away, not wanting anything to do with her or the children they'd fathered. Their money hadn't lasted, either; she'd used it to try to drown the visions and outrun the curse, both exercises in futility. She was ready to accept her fate.

But not her children's.

Her heart pounded as she watched those leather-bound arms wrap tight around her daughter, holding her close. Because he loved her? A tear trickled down Myra's cheek with her doubts. Ariel was beautiful. But she was cursed.

Giving them up hadn't saved her children; it had only prolonged the inevitable. Myra swayed, nearly toppling the chair, as a vision crashed through her mind: Ariel lying on a dirty cement floor, her turquoise eyes wide open but blinded…by death.

With a crack of static, the television blackened to a spark in the middle of the screen, swallowing the image of Ariel in David's arms. Ariel, curled in her favorite chair, lifted her head toward David, who held the remote in a tight fist. He'd just walked into her sunny yellow living room, dwarfing it with his size and presence. For better reception, he'd had to take his cell outside to phone the hospital. While he'd been gone, she'd received a call from the school board to suspend her.

"Is he all right?" she asked, her concern all for Ty. She'd deal with her pain later, by herself, as she always had.

He jerked his head in a short nod. "Yes. Twenty-two stitches later. But he lost a lot of blood. They're keeping him overnight."

"You should go. Be with him. I'm fine," she assured him. It wasn't the first time she'd lied to him. An old Gypsy proverb teased at her memory. *There are such things as false truths and honest lies.*

Her mother had used that proverb to justify how she'd made her living, traveling town to town conning people. Although only a child at the time she'd helped her mother, Ariel had known the staged séances and the phony crystal ball had been wrong. But her mother had insisted that sometimes it was better for people to hear lies than the truth; it hurt them less.

David tossed down the remote with such force that it bounced against the couch cushions, then he called her on the lie. "No, you're not fine. What were you thinking?"

Thinking? It didn't work that way. She didn't think. She just *saw.* Then she had to find a way to deal with what she'd seen. Numbness worked, but it always wore off too soon.

David didn't give her time to answer his question—even if she could—before he fired off another. "Do you know what could have happened to you?"

Shuddering, she crossed her arms over her chest, cupping her shoulders to still her trembling. She knew better than he did. Poor Haylee. The grief rushed in, squeezing her heart, but she refused to let the shock cripple her as it had at the crime scene. She squeezed her eyes shut, struggling against the mist.

Strong hands closed around her arms, pulling her out of the chair. David didn't enfold her in an embrace, just held her close enough so that their bodies brushed. Tension radiated from his long, hard frame. Usually Ariel melted against him whenever he touched her; today she stiffened, knowing that if she weakened, even a little, she would dissolve into a puddle of hysterical tears.

"That could be you, in the hospital, like Ty," he said, his voice vibrating with emotion. "Or worse, you could be in the morgue with that little girl."

"Haylee," she whispered her name.

"Oh, God…" He leaned over, touching his forehead to hers, with tenderness now, his anger spent. "I know and I'm so sorry, Ariel. You told me about her."

Her fears for the child. He'd adamantly supported her decision to trust her instincts and call social services, and when she'd met resistance to investigate Haylee's father over lack of resources and proof, David had intervened. He'd made sure someone had been sent out to the little girl's house, but that hadn't been enough.

"You tried to help her, Ariel."

She should have done more. She should have protected her even if she'd had to kidnap her and run away. Her heart clenched, hurting, and she blinked back the threatening tears. "I failed her." Maybe that was why the school board had suspended her.

"Her father did. Not you." He sighed, his ragged breath stirring her hair. "If you'd gotten there before Ty had, he could have killed you, too."

She shook her head. "I wasn't there long, David, just a little while before you."

"I wouldn't have been there at all if I hadn't seen you on the breaking news flash across my computer screen." He always had on the computer instead of the television because that was what he did—designed computers and software. He was Barrett, Michigan's answer to Bill Gates, as inventive, rich and powerful. But much more reclusive.

He hated media attention, but because of her, vans from local news stations currently blocked the street to his building. So he'd driven away from it and brought her home instead, to her little bungalow in a quiet, tree-lined burb of Barrett. Ariel would rather be here, inside the sunny yellow walls of her cheerful house. But its bright colors and tall, sun-filled windows couldn't cheer her today. Nothing could.

"Why didn't you call *me?*" he asked, his jaw taut.

"It was too late," she said, sighing. Even with all his money, he couldn't have done anything for Haylee.

Life was so damned unfair. What was the point of seeing ghosts when she couldn't do anything for them? She hadn't asked for this ability; she'd tried to ignore it. Anger rushed in, chasing away the last of her shock. She was ready to fight, to kick and hit something or someone, to lash out against the helplessness. Her hands clenched into fists.

"I could have been there with you, supporting you, protecting you. You shouldn't have gone by yourself," David said, his grip on her shoulders tightening.

She shivered, tempted to lean against him, to let his strong arms close around her and lift her burdens. But relying on someone was dangerous for Ariel; any time she had, she'd been hurt. In the six months they'd been dating, although David had always been attentive and caring, she couldn't trust that he'd always be there for her. No one else had. She could rely only on herself.

"I called Ty," she told him, but when he flinched, she realized he didn't need a reminder. She shrugged his hands off her shoulders and stepped around him, bristling. Anger was a defense mechanism. Hadn't one shrink or another told her that over the years? But like her ability to see ghosts, she couldn't suppress the feeling from bubbling up, so she lashed out, "That's what's really wrong! You're jealous!"

David's dark eyes narrowed as he studied her, assessing her as he might a computer glitch. "Ariel…"

"Is that the problem?" she asked, slinging the question like a slap. "That I called Ty instead of you?"

"The problem is," David said, his deep voice steady with reason, "that you went alone to a house where you know an abusive man lived. You put your life in danger."

"The police were there before I was." So had been the ambulance.

For Ty? Or for Haylee's father? She should have expected that the violent man would resist arrest. She never should have called Ty and put him in danger. He was David's best friend; that was probably why he'd flinched, over his friend getting hurt because of her. She should have called 911 instead. Ty hadn't even been on duty.

"So you called the police before you went over," David said, his jaw relaxing a bit as his tension eased. Then his dark eyes narrowed. "How did you know Haylee was in danger?"

She couldn't tell him about seeing the little girl's ghost and risk having David look at her as so many others had. Already he studied her, raising her defenses even more. He couldn't find out the truth or he'd reject her as everyone else had.

"You know I suspected abuse," she explained, hoping that would satisfy his sudden curiosity.

"Why didn't you call social services again?" he asked, his dark eyes intent on her face. "Why the police this time?"

"You know what social services did last time," she reminded him as bitterness joined her anger, churning in her stomach. "Nothing."

This time. Social services had taken her and her sisters away from her mom, and they'd never been in danger despite the unconventional lifestyle they'd lived. But for Haylee, with her sad eyes and fading bruises, they'd done nothing. Of course the child had been too frightened to tell them the truth about her home situation, about how since her mother had died, her father drank too much and beat her. She hadn't even told Ariel despite how close they'd grown, but Ariel had been able to figure it out. Why hadn't social services?

"How did you know something had happened to her?" David persisted.

She couldn't tell him how; he would never understand. None of the foster families with whom she'd lived growing up had understood that she was cursed. They'd thought her crazy instead. Some had told her so, others had just looked at her with pitying expressions, like the ones passersby cast at home-less people who ramble incoherently. She'd rather David be mad at her than look at her that way.

"Stop the inquisition already," she said, whirling away from him to stalk over to the windows. Through the gauzy white curtains she noticed a van with a satellite dish atop it parked across the street. Obviously they'd been followed. "You're worse than the reporters."

"Son of a bitch," he said, blowing out a ragged breath as he joined her at the window. "Damn vultures."

"Why do you hate the press so much?" Other businessmen might have enjoyed the free publicity. Not David.

His square jaw tautened as he peered through the curtain. "They're relentless, with no qualms over invading people's privacy."

And he was all about privacy. But then, so was Ariel. That need was one of the few things they had in common. The other was the attraction that hummed between them even now. Heat emanated from his body as he stood close behind her at the window. Even though inches separated them, it was as if he touched her. She could feel him against her skin, inside her heart.

"I'll call my security team, have someone run them off from the Towers." The high-rise in downtown Barrett that housed both his business and penthouse. He leaned closer, his breath warm against her neck. "I'll take you there."

"No." She didn't want to leave her cozy home for the cold, sterile building of glass, metal and marble where David lived.

"Ariel, you'll be safer there."

"Safe from whom?" The reporters wouldn't hurt her, at least not anymore, if it had been media coverage that had precipitated her suspension. The man who'd hurt Haylee was dead. The only one who could hurt her now was David. She shivered, uncertain of the origin of her errant thought. Sure, he was intense, but he would never harm her. Physically. If he knew the truth, he might hurt her emotionally. And he was getting too close, asking too many questions about how she'd known Haylee was in trouble.

The past several years she'd been careful to avoid getting deeply involved with anyone. She'd had her heart handed back to her so many times before that she'd promised she'd never give it away again. But

David hadn't asked for it, he'd just taken it. That was the kind of man he was, stronger and more powerful than any she'd known before.

"Ariel," he began, his deep voice soft with patience as he tried again to reason with her. "I have to get you away from the reporters. I don't want them harassing you."

"They're not the ones harassing me," she pointed out, turning away from the window.

He lifted his chin as if she'd physically slapped him this time. "And I am?"

"You're not helping. I lost a student, a precious little girl I cared about, and all you're doing is yelling at me and firing questions at me!" Or was she the one picking the fight? Her anger built, fueled by the nagging fear that he might learn the truth. "Do you care about me at all? Or are you just upset about the press coverage? Are you worried about *me* or your reputation?"

David's face paled as his eyes widened. "Ariel?"

He wasn't the only one shocked. She'd never talked to him like that, not once since she'd met him when Haylee had brought them together with a letter. Ariel had had all her students write one to David's company, requesting a computer donation for their struggling public elementary school. But it had been Haylee's letter praising her teacher that had compelled David to visit their classroom. That was all it had taken for Ariel to fall for him.

The blond Adonis with the brilliant mind and generous heart. She'd never met a man like him. He hadn't wanted any acknowledgment of the donation he'd made—enough computers not just for their small school but for the entire district. He'd only wanted her phone number. She'd given him so much more. Her heart. Now he would probably return it.

"Is that what you think of me?" he asked, his deep voice vibrating with hurt.

She pressed her palms to his hard chest as if to push him away, but as always, electricity arced between them, tingling in her veins as her blood rushed. All it ever took was one touch, sometimes just a look, for her to want him. What would she do if she lost him? If he walked away or, worse yet, left her as Haylee had? Fear gripped her, dredging up all the pain from her past. She couldn't go through that again. Not even for David. "David, I'm sorry—"

His hands skimmed down her back, pressing her tight against him. Then he tipped up her chin so she couldn't escape his dark gaze. "How can you think that I don't care about you? Haven't I shown you?"

He had. In so many ways. Not with his wallet—as would be easy for a man of his means—but with his time and attention, something few people had ever given Ariel. He called her, wishing her good mornings and good-nights. He sent her e-mails throughout the day telling her how beautiful she was inside and out, how much he respected her patience to teach little kids, how he couldn't wait to see her again. Even though he tried showing her how much she meant to him, she still doubted that *any* man could care about her if he really knew her and knew what she was.

He deserved the truth. But she couldn't risk giving him that. Besides rejecting her, besides thinking her crazy, he might think her a danger to herself. He was the kind of man who tried to protect others. What if he had her locked away, as some of her former foster parents had? Her heart lurched with fear and dread, and she blinked back tears. "David—"

His mouth came down on hers, silencing her. With sipping kisses, he coaxed her lips to open for him. But he only tasted her, his tongue just touching hers, before he pulled back and skimmed his lips across her jaw to the arch of her neck. Ariel bit her lip to hold back a moan as he nibbled, his teeth scraping lightly across her skin. Then he buried his face in her hair, his breath blowing hot and hard against her throat. Ariel shivered even as her blood rushed through her veins.

His chest rose and fell beneath her palms, tempting Ariel to peel away his black silk shirt to reveal the satin skin covering taut muscles. To slide her lips from his throat to his collarbone and lower. He always shuddered when she did that.

"How can you doubt me?" he whispered into her ear, his deep voice vibrating.

Because she doubted herself and her strength to survive another rejection. Her fingers knotted in his shirt, wrinkling the expensive fabric. She wanted to hold on to him, but unless he knew the truth, that wasn't fair…to either of them.

"I'm not good for you, David." Not in the way he deserved. He needed someone sweet and un-complicated. Someone uncursed.

"Are you talking about my reputation again?" he asked, pulling away from her.

Deprived of the heat of his embrace, she shivered again, this time as a foreboding chill raced across her skin. If he was worried about bad press now, what would happen if the media ever got wind of the past of the woman he was dating? He would have no privacy, no peace…until he distanced himself from her. Forever.

"I'm talking about your pride," she said, grasping at any excuse.

His forehead creased with confusion. "What?"

"Isn't that why you're upset I called Ty instead of you? It's why you hate publicity. You put your own pride before me," she accused, lifting her defenses again with anger as she tried to provoke his. She wanted him to walk away now…before she weakened so much she forgot her pride and begged him to stay.

He shook his head, his brow furrowed. "Why are you pushing me away?"

He was the one who'd pulled back physically. But emotionally she was doing as he accused, to protect herself as well as him. He was too good a man to live with her curse.

"If I'm pushing, why are you still here?" she asked, her heart aching as she struggled with her fears. "Just leave."

"Ariel?" Bewildered and hurt, his voice cracked on her name.

"Just leave me alone!" she shouted, all her anger and desperation raw and exposed in her shaking voice.

He drew in a ragged breath, and his chin lifted with the pride she'd accused him of putting before her. "If that's what you want, fine."

She closed her eyes, not opening them until the slam of the front door shook the thin walls of her house. She couldn't watch him walk away from her, not the way she'd watched Haylee fade into the mist. Once his temper calmed, he'd be back.

By then, she would be gone.

* * *

They circled him, these women cloaked in darkness with hooded robes covering their hair and shadowing their faces. Even as flames licked up from the blazing fire, they remained in shadow. The glow lit up the night sky while the smoke hung low, gathering thickly just above the ground, choking him. His lungs fought desperately for breath, and as he gasped and coughed, they laughed, their voices clear and melodious.

And malicious.

The laughter echoed in his ears, in his head, like thunder, splitting his skull. Pain throbbed at his temples, at his neck, radiating throughout his body until he shuddered under the force of it.

They were killing him. His chest ached as the last of his breath escaped him. The fire blurred, then burned on his lids as he closed his eyes on the life he'd known. But even then the pain wouldn't go away. There was no welcome release from it. No peace.

He jerked awake, throwing back the blankets tangled around him like the ropes with which they'd bound him. As he staggered from the bed, he bumped against the nightstand, knocking the journal to the cold, hard floor. The bang as the book struck the wood ricocheted like a gunshot through his skull.

Careful to move slowly as he bent over, he

reached for the journal. His family's history. His legacy, locked away for years, discounted as the incomprehensible ramblings of a crazy man. No one had understood his ancestor. Until now. Until just the few short weeks ago he'd come into possession of the journal and read it. If only he'd known sooner…about the curse, about the power of the charms and the witches. Now he understood his dreams, the black-and-white visions of his future. It was *his* curse. His demise.

If they got to him first.

But now that he knew about the witches and knew about their powers, he would be able to find them. To reclaim the charms and stop them.

To kill them before they killed him.

Chapter 2

The door opened at just the barest brush of her knuckles against the wood. A man stood in the shadow of the old oak door. Despite the two weeks that had passed, his face still bore traces of bruises in the yellow stains around his eyes and jaw. The same yellow Haylee had often worn, to match similar bruises.

"Ariel!" Ty said, his voice raspy either from disuse or from the bruises on his throat, visible even in the shadow of his shirt collar. "Where've you been?"

"Away." She'd run away, and she hated herself for the cowardice. She could have blamed her running on grief over Haylee, or despair over the school board suspending her. But she knew what it really was; like blood from a split lip, she could taste the fear.

"David's been going crazy looking for you. He's beyond worried."

No doubt he was furious, with every right. She'd taken off shortly after their fight, fleeing the shelter of her cozy little home for anonymous hotels. For an anonymous life. But she'd not been running from the media or from grief. She'd been running from herself, from who and what she was.

But like the times she'd run before—from the ghosts, from the disgust of foster parents—she'd realized there was no escape. She had to deal with what she was—and so would David once she gave him the chance. Fear over the risk she was taking squeezed her heart.

She hadn't told anyone about the curse since an old boyfriend back in college who'd dropped her and transferred to a different school after she'd shared her secret with him. After that heartbreak, she'd only casually dated. Until David.

"I'm sorry," she said. "I shouldn't have disappeared like that." Pushing David away before he could reject her had cheated them both.

Ty waved off her apology with a hand, the

knuckles of which were scabbed over, the fingers swollen. Then he stepped back and gestured her inside his apartment, one of three in a converted Tudor on Barrett's east side. Despite the cracks in the plaster and scratches on the old hardwood floors, the apartment was charming with its dark red paint, high ceilings, thick oak trim and leaded-glass windows. His living room expanded into the turret, bathing it in light, but somehow he remained in shadow.

"I'm not the one you need to apologize to," he said as he shoved his hands into the pockets of his faded jeans. "I'm not going crazy."

But his blue eyes were a bit wild, his manner more edgy than she'd ever seen him. She'd met Ty before she'd met David when the police officer had spoken at safety assemblies at the school. He'd definitely gotten through to the children about danger, intimidating more than befriending them. Like David, he was more intense than easygoing, his navy-blue eyes ever watchful. He always stared at her, making her wonder if she passed his scrutiny. Did he approve?

But this visit wasn't about her or David. "I'm apologizing to you," she insisted. "I never should have called you that day."

He shrugged. "What—you were going to dial 911 and explain that you wanted them to go out because a little kid missed school? Her dad called in the absence, saying she was sick. They wouldn't have sent anyone out."

"But you went." And for the first time she wondered why.

He jerked his chin down in a rough nod. "And if I hadn't, that bastard would have finished packing and skipped town. You did the right thing, Ariel, no matter what David said to you."

"You know?"

"That he was upset you called me?" He nodded again. "I've known David a long time." He chuckled, the sound rustier than his voice. "He's not too proud to admit to me when he's been an ass." His crooked grin faded. "He's really going crazy worrying about you."

"So he told you about the fight?" About what a bitch she'd been? If Ty had any sense, he would have told David to forget about her.

"Yeah, I agreed that he'd been an ass," he said with another rough laugh.

The muscles in Ariel's face twitched as she smiled for the first time in two weeks. "You're a good friend."

Ty's breath audibly caught. "Yeah, and that's too damned bad…."

Before she could ask what he meant, his door

rattled, shaking under the pounding of a fist. "Ty, you all right? I heard about the suspension…" David's last word trailed off as his friend opened the door. "Ariel!"

His dark eyes were shadowed, lines of fatigue rimming them. He'd apparently suffered as many sleepless nights as she had. He turned his gaze on Ty, his tone accusatory as he said, "You found her."

"Nobody found me," Ariel maintained. She was still lost, in so many ways.

David's gaze, full of heat and passion, swung back to her. The air between them crackled. "Ariel…"

"I was heading to the Towers," she insisted, resisting the urge to throw herself in his arms. She had run away when she'd needed him most and spent the past two weeks convincing herself she had to get used to being without him, that if he knew the truth he'd reject her. Assuming the worst hadn't been fair to either of them. "But I wanted to check on Ty first."

"You've checked. I'm fine," he said, his raspy voice dismissive. "You two can leave me alone."

Is that what he really wanted? She'd told David the same thing, but she hadn't been alone. She'd had Haylee, who'd stayed close to her, perhaps feeling Ariel's pain and knowing her teacher needed her. Mist funneled into the room; light warmed it, and

Haylee appeared, hovering at Ty's side. Did she think *he* needed her now, even more than Ariel did?

Ariel had David, if he still wanted her. From the way he stared at her, his eyes full of hunger and yearning, she suspected he did. But then, he didn't know yet what she had to tell him.

Ty cleared his throat, drawing David's attention to him. "Are you fine?" David asked him. "You've been suspended."

"Why?" Ariel gasped the question.

Ty's mouth twisted into a bitter grimace as he explained, "Man dies at the hands of an off-duty police officer. Internal Affairs has to investigate."

"You'll be cleared," David insisted, "and reinstated to active duty soon."

Ty shrugged as if he didn't care. Ariel didn't know him well, but she knew enough about Ty to realize that his job was his life. Losing it would kill him.

She could identify. Her heart ached for her second graders. Not only had they lost a classmate—someone they'd all loved—but their teacher had been taken away from them, too. Tears threatened; she missed them so much.

At least she could still see Haylee, faintly, as her image began to fade into the mist. Both men, intuitive, insightful men, were blind to what she saw, the light and the child.

"I'm sorry," she said to Ty again.

"Same thing happened to you." Ty revealed his knowledge of her.

"I talked to the principal," David admitted. "I'll talk to the board next."

"Don't," Ariel said, knowing that he wanted to fix things for her. But there were things that even his money and influence couldn't fix.

"You're not ready to go back to work," he surmised as his dark eyes asked another question. Was she ready to go back to *him?*

"Would you two like me to take off?" Ty asked, either with generosity or bitter irony. His raspy voice distorted his tone and his blue eyes guarded his emotions.

"No," Ariel was quick to reply.

"We'll leave?" David worded his response as a question, asked of Ariel, not Ty.

She stepped closer to him and nodded. "I'll meet you at your penthouse." Then she added in a whisper, "Give me a minute alone with Ty?"

Some dark emotion passed through his eyes, making her shiver as if a cold wind had blown into the apartment. But he nodded, then glanced at Ty over her head. "We'll talk later." His deep voice vibrated with a warning. About Ty's suspension or about her?

The door shut hard, just short of a slam, behind

him as David left them alone. Ty blew out a heavy breath. "Sometimes he forgets that I'm not one of his employees."

David didn't treat Ty like an employee, though. He treated him more like a brother. Underneath the bossiness there was affection. After she'd been separated from her family, Ariel had known little affection in her life.

"Why are you friends?" she wondered aloud, then felt heat rush to her face. "I don't mean that in a derogatory way. It's just that you have nothing in common."

Except their intensity.

Half of Ty's bruised mouth lifted into a crooked grin. "Oh, you'd be surprised."

"Seriously." She wanted to know. In the six months she'd been with David, their friendship had fascinated her. She'd never experienced anything like the bond between them. Not even her family had been that close, not as close as she'd like to remember. If they had, someone would have found her by now. Despite the times she'd run away, she'd always come back to Barrett. She hadn't changed her name; she'd waited for them to come find her. But no one had looked. No one had cared.

"Seriously?" Ty repeated, lifting an eyebrow

creased with a thin scar. He sighed before sharing his succinct answer, "History."

"History?" She smiled at his odd response. "You mean because you were friends for such a long time?"

Ty sighed. "It's more complicated than that. David's never told you?"

Her lips turned back down; she didn't feel like smiling anymore. "Told me what?"

Ty's blue gaze was ever watchful, his tone curious as he asked, "How much do you know about him?"

Not nearly enough, apparently, but she'd always thought she knew more than he did about her. "Of course you're going to know more than I do about David. It's not like we've been dating for years," she defended her ignorance.

And it wasn't as if they spent all their time talking when they were together. So much of their communication required no words. Only kisses, caresses… moans of pleasure. If there was something about him she needed to know, she was certain David would have told her. *She* was the one keeping secrets.

"No, it's not," Ty agreed, rubbing a hand along his jaw darkened with stubble as well as the shadow of the bruises from Haylee's father's fists.

Ty had said that Haylee's father had died resisting arrest. Based on media accounts, during the ensuing fight, Mr. Reynolds had sustained a blow to the head that had killed him. She knew what had happened, but there was something else she had to know.

"*Why* did you go that day?" she asked.

He shrugged his broad shoulders as if it were no big deal. "You asked me to."

"But I didn't give you a reason." Because she couldn't. She couldn't tell *him* how she'd known that something horrible had happened to Haylee. She'd have to tell David first. "Did you trust my…instincts?"

His blue eyes unblinking, he stared intently at her. "I trusted *you*."

She drew in a quick little breath. "I need to go."

He nodded. "To David." This time she caught the bitterness in his voice and eyes as he held open the door for her to leave. What was the history between these two supposedly best friends? And why was she suddenly afraid to learn it?

She walked over the threshold, then stopped and turned back as she said again, "I'm sorry."

"Me, too," he said before closing the door in her face and shutting her out.

Had David shut her out of some part of his life, of his past? If so, she needed to learn it from him, not his friend. But now she wondered…why had he, a powerful man used to getting what he wanted, let her push him away two weeks ago? Maybe he didn't want her. Or maybe she wasn't the only one keeping secrets.

* * *

Ariel shivered under the cold stare of the security guard standing inside the opulent marble and brass lobby of the Towers. The glass-and-chrome high-rise was actually named *Koster* Towers, after the man who'd built it. The man she wanted to see, if security would let her. Like David, the guard was a big man, but he had graying hair and pale eyes. Although he studied her as if he'd never seen her before, he knew who she was. Why make the play of requesting her driver's license, then phoning the penthouse to see if she were allowed up?

David took a long time to respond to the guard, but after the way he'd acted at Ty's, she doubted he'd changed his mind about wanting to see her. At least she hoped he hadn't.

Ariel's heart thumped slow and hard as it lay heavy in her chest. In the two weeks she'd been gone, she'd come to some important realizations. The first, of course, had been that she couldn't run from who she was anymore. The second had been that she needed David in her life. She couldn't say that without him it wouldn't be worth living; she'd never had any problem going on alone.

But she didn't want to anymore. She wanted David at her side and she wanted to be at his…if she were ever allowed to see him. Her palm itched, tempting her to slam it against the marble counter over which the guard loomed. But then the man jerked his chin toward the private elevator. His voice gruff, he conceded, "You can go up now."

She followed the Oriental runner to the elevator, stepping inside the small car of mirror and brass. Before she could press any buttons, the doors swished closed and the car jerked, beginning its ascent. She stared at the image reflected at her. Red hair, long and tangled, falling around a face devoid of makeup. A loose-knit brown sweater hung on her, like the long denim skirt, the tattered hem dangling threads against her brown leather boots.

No wonder the guard had questioned her admittance to the penthouse. She undoubtedly didn't appear suitable for a man of David's wealth and power. But David never cared how she dressed; he always called her beautiful. The guard probably watched her from cameras hidden somewhere inside the elevator. She considered sticking out her tongue but resisted the urge. Obviously she'd been spending too much time around second graders. Or she once had. After she settled things with David, she'd see about getting her job back or getting another. She missed teaching almost as much as she'd missed him.

The car shuddered to a halt, and her stomach

lifted, not from the height but with nerves. Would he forgive her running away? She hadn't even taken her cell phone when she'd left, so he'd had no way to contact her.

The doors slid open to the two-story foyer of the penthouse. A wide mahogany staircase wound up one corner of it while plaster columns separated the sitting area from the hall leading to the rest of the apartment.

"David?" she called out as she stepped out of the elevator. "David?"

Her heels clinked against the marble floor like wineglasses in a toast as she walked across the foyer. Light glowed from the living room, so she followed it through the rows of plaster columns, down a couple marble steps until she neared what David called the conversation pit, where black leather couches angled around an octagonal table in front of a massive marble fireplace. Despite the warmth of the spring day, a fire burned in the hearth, mirroring the flames of the profusion of candles arranged on the glass-top table.

"David?" she said as she neared the couches. Along with the candles, a bouquet of red roses adorned the table, the flames reflecting in its crystal vase making it look as if the stems were on fire.

"You're here," he said as he joined her in the living

room. He carried a silver tray laden with flutes of sparkling champagne and plates of canapés.

"As if you didn't know," she said. "I couldn't get past the lobby until you authorized it. Did you take me off the list?"

"List?" His mouth kicked into a secretive grin. "You think I have a list."

She nodded, refusing to be distracted by his handsome face. She loved that wicked grin, loved the creases it left in his cheeks, the way it warmed his dark eyes. "And I'm not on it anymore."

He gestured at the table, the candles, then the fire burning in the hearth. "I might have asked the guard to stall you."

"So you could set this scene?"

For what? Seduction? It never took him much for that. Just that grin. The touch of his hand. The brush of his lips. Her stomach quivered as heat spread throughout her body. Since she stood before the hearth, she would blame the warmth of the fire, but she knew better. David got her hot. Her body craved his almost to the point of obsession.

"Is it working?" he asked her as he set the tray on the table next to the candles. Then he pushed aside her hair to brush his lips against the nape of her neck. Her pulse quickened. He didn't miss her reaction, as he chuckled and asked, "Should I stoke the fire?"

With another kiss, another touch?

"You must be cold," he said.

She had been cold and alone, even with Haylee's sweetness haunting her. "I missed you," she admitted.

"Good," he said, his voice hard.

She glanced up in surprise at his harsh tone and turned toward him. "David?"

"I was going out of my mind worrying about you, wondering where you were—" his hands settled onto her shoulders, tangling in her hair "—wanting you at my side."

Instead of feeling guilt, satisfaction lifted her spirits. He cared as much as she did. She smiled. "So I heard."

"From Ty?" His brown eyes darkened with emotion. Bitterness or resentment? Or something else?

"Is it a problem that I stopped there first?" She probably wouldn't have if she hadn't been stalling on carrying out the decision she'd made to tell David everything.

He shook his head, tousling his golden hair. "Not at all. I'm worried about Ty, too."

"Why?" she asked. "The suspension?"

David sighed. "It's more than that."

"He's healing all right?"

"Physically, yes," he replied. "I've checked with

his doctors." To whom patient-doctor confidentiality obviously meant nothing. But when David Koster asked a question, people answered him. Except her. She'd done a good job avoiding telling him anything about her past. She hadn't realized he'd done the same to her.

"So what are you worried about?" she asked. "His emotional well-being?"

"All Ty has to do for reinstatement is talk to a psychiatrist. Then he'd be cleared to return to duty."

"But he won't do it." She couldn't blame him. After she'd been taken away from her mother, she'd been forced to talk to a barrage of psychologists. The minute any foster family had learned about her ability, she'd been sent to one. A couple of times she'd even been locked away in a psychiatric ward, with other kids screaming and yelling or laughing maniacally.

David's hands slid from her shoulders, and he walked a few paces away. "No, he won't."

"Maybe he's not ready to talk about that day." Sometimes it was better if a person didn't share everything. Maybe she shouldn't tell David. Just talking about psychologists reminded her how anyone who'd learned the truth had looked at her as if she were crazy.

"It's not just *that day* he's avoided talking about,"

David remarked with another ragged sigh as he stared moodily into the fire.

"History," she said, admitting to the knowledge of their bond.

He turned to her and blinked as if clearing something from his mind. "What?"

"History," she repeated, wondering why he'd been distracted. "You and Ty share quite a past."

His eyes darkened and his jaw clenched. "What did he tell you?"

"Nothing." And she had an eerie suspicion that neither would David. "I just know that you two have been friends a long time."

"Yes," David admitted. "We grew up together." The hard edge to his tone suggested that he wasn't talking about just chronological years but something else, something that had caused them to grow up faster. "He even lived with us…after his dad died."

Fathers meant little to her. She'd never known hers. Undoubtedly Daddy Dearest had been rich; her mother had liked the security of rich men. Even at nine Ariel had realized that. Now, looking back from a woman's perspective, she also realized her father had probably been married. He'd certainly never been any part of their lives. Neither had Elena's father or Irina's. Since their mother had lied for money, she'd undoubtedly cheated, too. But that was long ago and should matter nothing to Ariel anymore.

All that mattered now was David.

But she found herself asking about Ty. "His mom was already gone?" Dead or just lost to him, as Ariel's was lost to her? Perhaps that was why Ty had come when she'd called; they had the unspoken bond of abandoned children. Maybe she should have told Ty about her past first; his acceptance might have come more easily than David's.

David nodded. "She died when he was about five."

At least *his* mother had an excuse for being gone. "Then he lost his dad, too?"

A muscle twitched in David's jaw, he clenched it so hard. "That was more a blessing than a curse."

She winced at first the word, then the sentiment. "David!"

"His dad was a monster," he explained. "Used to beat the hell out of Ty."

"Like Haylee's father did her." That was why Ty had gone when she'd called him.

"God, Ariel, I'm sorry about bringing that up," David said. "I shouldn't have…."

She shook her head. "No, *I* shouldn't have. I shouldn't have called Ty." He was the last person she should have called. "All those memories must have come rushing back—"

"Not for the first time," David pointed out. "Ty's been in that situation before since becoming a police officer, and you had no way of knowing about his past."

"Because you hadn't told me," she reminded him. "We don't know much about each other's pasts." She drew in a shaky breath. Was she ready to tell him?

"We have time to learn," he said, closing his big hands over her shoulders again.

"Do we?" she wondered aloud.

"Give me another chance, Ariel. I was an ass." He moved his hands from her shoulders to her neck, holding her face, with his thumbs stroking along her jaw.

She shivered at his light touch. "David—"

"Forgive me." He didn't ask for her forgiveness, he demanded it.

She could not deny him. She reached up and linked her arms around his neck. "I already have. If you forgive me…"

"Forgive you what?" he asked as he pulled her closer. He slid his hands over her back, the heat from his palms branding her even through the thickness of her chenille sweater.

"Yelling at you," she reminded him. "Taking off without telling you where I was going."

"Did you know where you were going?"

She shook her head, tangling her hair around his fingers. "I just needed to get away." If not for her feelings for him, she might not have returned.

"You were devastated," he said, his voice heavy with regret and sympathy. "I should have been more sensitive."

She gestured toward the fire, the candles and the champagne. "You are."

"Now. I wasn't then when you needed sensitivity most," he said, his voice heavy with self-condemnation. "I was just so scared that you could have been hurt. The thought of losing you…" His breath shuddered out, and his arms tightened even more. "I *can't* lose you, Ariel."

Pressed tight against his hard body, Ariel could feel each beat of his heart and every breath he took. She trembled with the desire to be part of him. Always. "Why, David?"

"I need you in my life. I know we haven't been together long, but *that* day—and the past two weeks—made me realize something."

Nerves fluttered in her stomach. She had to swallow twice before asking, "What did you realize, David?"

He drew back and cupped her face again, his hands gentle as he cradled her jaw. "I love you, Ariel."

Her heart lifted, but out of self-preservation she squashed the hopefulness. In the past people had claimed to love her, but all of them had eventually abandoned her. She didn't need the *words* from him, she needed action, proof of his love. And the only way she'd have that was if she tested him…with the truth.

But she didn't know where to begin. "David…"

He winced, as if her hesitation physically hurt him. "I know after the way I acted that you must have your doubts about us. But I'll make it up to you," he vowed, "if you give me the chance, Ariel. Say yes."

"Yes?"

He released her and stepped back, then dropped to one knee in front of her and the fire. "Marry me."

Again, not a request but a demand. From a man who was used to getting what he wanted. But would he want her once he learned the truth? She had to tell him, but she couldn't look at him, couldn't face the expression that might cross his face. The way his eyes might widen first with disbelief, then darken with disappointment and regret, then, worst of all, pity. She stared into the fire as she began, "David, I need to…"

"To think about it?" he finished for her. "I'll give you as much time as you need, Ariel. But while you think about it, I want you to wear this." He slid something cold and hard onto her finger, drawing

Ariel's attention to her hand. A diamond, square and bright, twinkled up at her, aglow with the reflection of flames.

She drew in a quick breath. "It's beautiful." And, knowing David, very expensive. She couldn't fathom how many carats, nor did she care. The ring meant nothing to her; it was the man she didn't want to lose.

No windows were open, but it was as if a wind blew through the room. The candles burned higher and brighter. The flames in the hearth kicked up to tall spires of vivid orange. Ariel grabbed David's shoulders, pulling him back as if he might get burned.

"Ariel, what's wrong?" His voice was faint, the fire roaring louder, deafening.

Smoke filled the room, thicker and more impenetrable than any mist she'd ever seen. Unlike the mist, the smoke carried a scent, not of burning wood but of sandalwood incense and lavender. The flames rose even higher, taking shape. The shape of a woman. A woman Ariel hadn't seen in twenty years. The woman's dark eyes burned with fire, her long, curly black hair turning to lava and her mouth open in a scream that Ariel couldn't hear…she could only see.

Ariel smothered the scream rising to her lips and tried to still her sudden trembling. *Mama?* She was older now, twenty years older than when Ariel had last seen her, the night she and her sisters had been taken away and placed into separate foster homes. Her mother had never once sought them out in all those years. Had never once tried to reunite them or even see Ariel. She was only the first of many who had rejected Ariel over the past twenty years. But her rejection had hurt the most.

Resentment rose in a familiar bitter wave of nausea in Ariel's stomach. But she swallowed it down with the scream, knowing she had no outlet for those feelings. She would never be able to express them now. It was too late.

The flames grew brighter, the image shifting but never vanishing as her mother danced with the fire. Dread settled heavily over Ariel's heart, and she accepted what she saw.

Her mother appeared to her as so many others had throughout Ariel's life. Her secret was that she could see the ghosts of those who had recently passed away. Being called crazy was the least of her concerns now, as tears burned her eyes and trickled down her cheeks. Her mother was dead. The last words Ariel had said to her played through her mind with stunning clarity. *Mama, I'm cursed....*

The cloaked figures danced around the fire, moving in and out of the flames. He didn't fear them now. He controlled them. He told them what to do. The power was *his*.

But he wanted more. Killing one of the witches wasn't enough. He needed to kill them all and reclaim the little pewter charms. The woman had sworn that she hadn't given them to her children, but he'd known she lied. He'd heard her think it and had seen the flash of her memory as she passed one to each of her three daughters, giving them power. Power that belonged to him.

He opened his eyes, wincing at the light even though it shone softly through the green shade, casting an eerie glow around his office. He reached across his desk, closing his slightly trembling fingers around the pewter edge of a trifold picture frame. In his vision, the hoods of their dark brown robes concealed their faces, but he knew what they looked like now. Or at least what they'd looked like twenty years ago, the blonde, the redhead and the little one who was the very image of her gypsy mother. Witches, all of them.

His fingers tightened around the frame until his knuckles whitened. A couple more witches than these lived, taunting him. They would have to die, too. But these girls were the ones he most needed to find, these were the ones with the charms.

He had held this frame often just in the short time

he'd come into possession of the picture of three young girls. Had *she?* Had she looked into the faces of her lost children? Had she wondered, as he did now, where the hell they were?

But it wouldn't take him long. Finding people was easy. They could change their names, their identities; it made it a little harder to track them down than those who hadn't. But it didn't matter.

In the end, he would find them. In fact, he was pretty certain he already knew where one was, had already gotten close to her, close enough to kill. But he wanted all of the sisters, not just one.

He closed his eyes on their young faces as pain shot through his skull. He needed the charms. He needed their power if he was going to survive. Blindly he reached inside a desk drawer, passing over the flimsy plastic of a prescription bottle for the metal flask. Even the soft scrape of unscrewing the cap reverberated inside his head. He winced, took a sip of the fiery liquid and winced again.

Fire. That was how the first one had died, the flames consuming her as they had her ancestor over three hundred and fifty years ago. He would kill the others in equally suitable ways befitting witches.

Chapter 3

Ariel avoided cemeteries and never attended funerals. But she couldn't forgive herself for not going to Haylee's. She owed her that much because she'd failed her so dismally otherwise. She shouldn't have counted on social services to save the little girl; she knew better. She should have done it herself by kidnapping her and taking her away. But then she would have had to give up David. The irony was that she still might when he learned the truth.

Her heart heavy with guilt and regret, she drove to Barrett's cemetery, intent on paying her respects at the child's grave. Once there, parked along one of the tree-lined streets winding through the plots, dread rose like nausea in her stomach. Her hands shaking, she reached for the handle on the driver's door, forcing herself to step from the Jeep.

The mist swirled in, not quite as thick as it had the night before, and the light shone brightly through it without the orange glow of the flames. Many images hovered in the mist, ghosts of those departed from this world but not entirely ready for what lay beyond. At least that was why Ariel assumed she could see them—because they hadn't entirely left. And here, in a cemetery, their bodies were buried but not their souls. Ariel could see their souls, so many souls.

Her head grew light, overwhelmed by all the pale faces and nearly transparent bodies. All their mouths moved, speaking words she couldn't hear. Mama had always said Ariel needed to learn to listen. Ariel had thought that might have been why her mother had let authorities take her children— because Ariel had never listened. And Elena had been stubborn and willful. And Irina…

There was no reason why her mother let them take Irina. She'd been such a sensitive little girl. Haylee, with her big, dark eyes and long curls, reminded Ariel so much of her little sister. Because of that resemblance and the child's sweetness, they'd forged a bond deeper than that of teacher and student.

Ariel carried a bouquet of daisies to where a champagne-colored marble stone marked a fresh grave. Haylee must have had some other family, because someone had paid for the elaborate stone, intricately engraved with an angel heralding the years of Haylee's birth and death. Below her name was the phrase *Sweet child, forever an angel*. Tears burned Ariel's eyes, blurring the words. "I'm so sorry, Haylee."

Through the mist the little girl appeared, shaking her head, denying Ariel any blame. Even without words, Ariel could understand the child, but she couldn't understand her mother. Why had she appeared in the fire the other night at the moment of David's proposal?

Had she just died? That was usually when the spirits first appeared to Ariel, soon after their deaths. But that wasn't always the case, because she could see so many lost souls in the cemetery, and the only fresh grave was Haylee's. Ariel really had no idea how her "gift" worked. Maybe if she could hear what the ghosts tried to tell her, she would understand. But she couldn't. So it really was more a curse than a blessing.

If her mother hadn't just died, she must have had

some reason to appear to Ariel. Had she come to warn her about something? Since her forced leave from teaching, Ariel had nothing going on in her life. Nothing but David.

If her mother had come to warn her about him, Ariel hadn't heeded her. She glanced down at the diamond adorning her finger. Her hand should ache from the size of the square stone, her eyes hurt from its brilliance. Technically she hadn't accepted the proposal and had only agreed to wear the ring while she considered it. From the flash of pain in his dark eyes, David didn't understand that her hesitance had nothing to do with him and everything to do with her. She'd intended to share everything with him…until she'd seen her mother's ghost.

As she stared down at the diamond, the mist thickened, becoming more smoke than fog, carrying that faint scent of sandalwood and lavender. The light turned eerily orange. Even before she glanced up, she knew Haylee was gone, replaced by the image of her mother.

"Mama, what do you want?" Now. After all these years of no contact, no concern. "I've been here." Waiting for her. "Why didn't you come sooner?" When Ariel could have heard her words and understood what she wanted.

The woman's arms moved, flailing, almost as if

shoving Ariel away. But she'd already done that long ago. Was she urging her to leave again?

Ariel was done running. She couldn't escape who and what she was. A Durikken woman, both gifted and cursed. Like her mother.

"Mama, I'm sorry...."

The woman reached out again, as if to wipe the tears from her daughter's face. But Ariel could feel only the barest brush of air against her cheek. Her mother's image faded along with the light and the smoke.

Smoke. Had Mama died in a fire? One someone had set...like the one that had started that vendetta so long ago? Even though she'd been young when her mother had shared the legend with them, Ariel remembered it well, maybe because it was her last memory of her mother and sisters, in that cramped little camper with candles burning as Mama had talked of special abilities and vengeance. Vengeance had been sworn on all the descendants of that witch; they'd been cursed to die violent deaths.

Ariel shuddered. She'd almost convinced herself that she'd invented the story, maybe as a coping device to deal with the separation from her mother and sisters. No parent would have told a child such a story, one that had given Ariel nightmares even years later. She fumbled with her bracelet, clutching the worn pewter charm. Heat flowed from it through her fingertips. It was real. All of it. Her mother's story. The legend. The vendetta. Because of the charm, she knew it was true.

Even now she could remember the way her mother's voice had trembled with fear as she'd told them of her ancestor's death. Is that how Myra had died? Burned to death?

Pain clenched Ariel's heart. "Oh, Mama…"

For just an instant the orange glow grew, beckoned, then disappeared entirely. If the vendetta had been resurrected, that meant that Ariel and her sisters would be in danger, that they could be killed, too.

Fear rushed in, but the sensation wasn't new. She had lived with fear since that night so many years ago when her mother had shared the legend and Ariel had lost her family. Now she could lose her life. And so could her sisters.

Hands shaking, she dropped the daisies on Haylee's grave and ran to the Jeep. She wasn't sure where she was driving until she stopped outside the massive dark brick building that housed the offices for the city of Barrett, including Child Protective Services. She tightened her fingers around the steering wheel to still their trembling. This place had brought her nothing but pain and frustration, but that was the least of her concerns now. Impatience gnawed at her as she pulled her car behind the line waiting for admittance to the parking ramp. When her turn came, she ripped off the ticket and barely waited for the gate to lift before driving into the darkness of the concrete structure. Even at noon, light was minimal in the garage. But Ariel wasn't scared of the dark; she had far worse things to fear.

She squeezed her Jeep Cherokee into a spot designated for small cars, threw open the door, then shut it so hastily that it barely closed. She rushed into the stairwell, passing others on their way down for lunch. But she needn't have worried that the person she wanted to see had left. The social worker Ariel sought sat at her desk, distractedly pulling crackers from a sandwich bag as she studied a file.

Ariel just stood there for a minute, near the woman's desk, catching her breath. Not from her quick ascent of the stairs, but from the emotions rushing through her. Seeing this woman brought back painful ones. Ariel's eyes burned, and she blinked against the glare of the fluorescent lights, so bright in contrast to the darkness of the parking garage and stairwell.

This social worker wasn't the one who'd taken Ariel and her sisters away from her mom. Margaret was probably only in her thirties; she'd not been at the job so long that she was burned out or didn't care. But neither had she been able to help Haylee despite the interviews she'd conducted.

Would she help Ariel?

"Margaret."

The woman closed her eyes a moment before looking up, but she wasn't able to conceal her feelings from Ariel, her sadness, her guilt. They haunted her dark eyes the way the ghosts haunted Ariel. Lines of stress and exhaustion wrinkled her black skin, adding years to her pretty face.

Ariel's heart softened, tempting her to assuage the woman's regret with kind words, to tell her that she'd done all she could. But Ariel couldn't. To get the information she needed, she intended to use that guilt. She'd deal with her own later…after she knew her sisters were safe.

"Miss Cooper—"

"Ariel. Please call me Ariel."

"You weren't so friendly the last time we talked," the social worker reminded her.

Ariel sighed. "I was frustrated. I wanted you to do more for Haylee."

"I tried," the woman insisted, her voice catching with emotion. "I wish I could have."

"You're not the only one," Ariel admitted, her heart heavy with so many regrets.

"You didn't even come to her funeral," the social worker said, her gaze hard with recrimination.

Ariel hung her head, straining the tense muscles at the back of her neck. "I couldn't...I just...couldn't."

"It was hard," Margaret said, sighing. "I didn't figure on anyone else being there...except for you and me."

"So you were the only one." Tears of regret burned Ariel's eyes. Haylee had deserved a better send-off than a lone mourner.

"No," Margaret said, confusion wrinkling her forehead. "Your fiancé was there."

"My fiancé?"

Margaret nodded toward Ariel's hand. "Figured he'd come across with quite the rock. He's a generous man, paying for the funeral and the monument."

David. Of course he had been the one to take care of the arrangements. Ariel swallowed hard. "Yes, he is."

"A girl dreams about landing a man like that," the woman added with a deep sigh.

Landing? Ariel hadn't sought him out; she wasn't entirely like her mother. His money meant nothing to her. "David's wonderful," she agreed. He deserved someone so less complicated than her, but she couldn't summon the selflessness to let him go.

"Since you weren't at the funeral, I didn't think I'd be seeing you again," the social worker remarked.

"I wouldn't be here if I didn't need your help." Ariel deliberately added the next word, hating herself for the manipulation. "Again."

Pain flashed through Margaret's eyes; they both knew she hadn't helped Ariel last time. "Are you here to file a report about another student?"

"No. This is personal."

The woman leaned back in her chair. It must have been old because it creaked despite her slight weight. Ariel had the feeling that the woman didn't eat much, probably just those crackers at her desk. "Personal?" Margaret asked. "I thought you had no children."

"I don't. It's about me."

Margaret's full lips tilted into a slight smile as she handed a Child Protective Services card across the desk. "This is the name of the services we offer. You're pretty young, but you're no child."

She hadn't been one since she was nine. "And I can protect myself," she pointed out, forcing a smile. She wasn't the only one she intended to protect. She had to find her sisters, to warn them that the vendetta may have been resurrected. They needed to be aware of whatever danger may be stalking them.

Margaret's forehead wrinkled again. "Then I don't understand…."

"I have a file here," she admitted.

The social worker's eyes widened with surprise. "You were in the system?"

"Since I was nine."

"Here? In Barrett?"

She nodded. "It must have been the closest place with child services."

"I was twelve when I got in the system," Margaret shared.

They had more in common than Haylee's tragedy. This woman would understand. Ariel began, "I need some information."

Margaret shook her head. "I've got a feeling this isn't the first time you've asked."

"When I was eighteen." Emotions crashed through her as she fought against the memory, but she couldn't force it away. She'd been so young and, even after the life she'd lived, naive. She'd thought then that it would be easy to find her mother and sisters. So she'd been hopeful, but she'd also been scared of what seeing them again might do to her, that it might increase her power, her ability to see dead people. And she'd been scared of what it might do to them, remind them of all they'd left behind—the crazy, vagabond existence and the vendetta—and that they'd hate her for disrupting their lives.

She needn't have feared anything then. Her mother
hadn't just had her children taken from her, she'd
given them up, signing away all her parental rights.
Elena and Irina had been adopted, their names
changed. Ariel had been the only one nobody wanted.
Pain clasped her heart in tight fists, squeezing until
she lost her breath a moment. Then she glanced down
at her hand, catching the sparkle of David's diamond
under the glare of the fluorescent lights. David
wanted her. But when he knew the truth…

"So you know what's in your file," Margaret said,
lifting her shoulders in a shrug.

Yes, Ariel knew. Given up by her mother. Shuf-
fled from foster home to foster home due to psy-
chotic episodes. "I'm not interested in my file."

Margaret's eyes widened. "You want me to let
you look at someone else's?"

Ariel glanced around the open area; most of the
desks were empty. Unlike Margaret, many of her
coworkers probably ate out, needing to get away for
a little while. Ariel preferred to think that was where
they were, rather than out investigating more claims.
"No one has to know. I wouldn't be asking you unless
it was really important." A matter of life and death.

Margaret bit her bottom lip, as if she were con-
sidering it. "That's all you want…"

Then we'll be even? Margaret didn't say that, but

Ariel heard it and wondered how anything could even out the loss of a little girl's life. Maybe saving some other lives…

"When I was taken away from my mom, so were my two sisters. I need to know where they are."

"You tried before…when you were eighteen?"

Ariel nodded. "Their names got changed. I can't find them on my own." Not that she had tried all that hard. After learning her mom had given them up, she'd been too stung by rejection to keep searching for her or them. She'd been convinced they'd want nothing to do with her. Undoubtedly that hadn't changed, but maybe they would at least listen to her warning. She had to try. "Please…"

"I don't know." Margaret sighed, a ragged expulsion of air. "If anyone found out, it could be my job…."

Ariel shook her head. "I'd never ask, but…I'm pretty desperate here." And she wasn't too proud to admit it.

"What year did you enter the system?"

"1986. My mother's name was Myra Cooper."

"Was?"

"I haven't seen her since." Not alive. Ariel glanced around, searching for the smoke or mist. But neither ghost had followed her here, to this place, where she most needed comfort and reassurance.

"What about your sisters?" Margaret asked.

Ariel shook her head again. "Their names are Elena and Irina." Were. She didn't know what they called themselves now. Were they married? Did they have children? She couldn't consider the bigger question. Surely she would have seen them if they were...

"1986." Margaret bit her lip again. "That'd be in dead storage."

She didn't know the half of it.

The social worker stood up and picked up her bag of crackers, handing them across the desk to Ariel. "Help yourself. I'll be right back."

Was it that easy? The pain and disappointment of the last time she tried to find her family flashed through her. She'd waited nine long years, confident the information would be hers once she turned eighteen. But it hadn't worked that way then. And the longer she waited for Margaret, the more she got that sick feeling—the rising nausea, the pounding headache—that it wouldn't work that way now either.

The woman came back empty-handed. She settled onto the chair behind her desk but wouldn't look at Ariel. Her gaze stayed on her computer monitor, but the screen was dark.

"You found *my* file," Ariel said, fighting to keep the accusation from her voice. And she had read it. Margaret knew what those foster families had said about her, what her caseworker had thought. And now she was so disgusted she couldn't even look at Ariel. "What about my sisters? Did you find their files?"

The social worker clearly didn't trust Ariel anymore; like all those other people, she thought Ariel was crazy. "I can't give you any information about them. They were adopted."

Ariel knew that. "I need to find them." Should she tell the woman why? Margaret already thought Ariel crazy, so what did she have to lose? But somehow she didn't think the truth would help her.

Margaret shook her head. "I *can't* help you." Before she'd read Ariel's file, she'd been willing to bend rules for her. Not now.

Hands shaking, Ariel set the bag of crackers back on the woman's desk. Maybe she should have eaten some; they might have settled the nausea in her stomach.

Margaret cleared her throat, probably uncertain how to speak to Ariel now, the way most people were uncertain or reluctant to talk to people with questionable sanity. Finally she advised, "Leave the past where it belongs."

Dead storage.

"They're my sisters."

"Yeah, well, we both know blood's not really that thick." Meaning she thought, as Ariel had, that they

would reject her. "You could be opening yourself up
for a world of hurt. You have a good thing going. You
landed Barrett's most eligible bachelor."

It never occurred to Ariel that people might think
she was with David for his money. Would he think
that when he knew the truth? When he knew that her
mother had gone after men for their money? Or had
it been the security their money had offered,
because she'd always been running from a three-
hundred-and-fifty-year-old vendetta?

Ariel understood everything now, why her mother
had never stayed in one place for very long. She'd
been running for her life…and theirs. Ariel didn't
doubt the veracity of the legend; it wasn't a story her
mother had told the way other mothers read their
children fairy tales. Having seen the smoke and the
flames and the fear in her mother's dead eyes, Ariel
knew beyond any niggling doubt that the vendetta
was real. She hoped her sisters would, too, when she
found them. She trembled as the fear with which
she'd lived for so long increased.

"I need to know," Ariel beseeched her, leaning
forward to whisper as some people had filed back
into the offices, "where my sisters are."

"I didn't even pull their files," Margaret whispered back. "I'm telling you to leave it alone."

Leave *them* alone. She couldn't. Not until she

knew they were safe. "I should have known you wouldn't help me." She didn't feel that guilty this time when she added, "Again."

Margaret bit her bottom lip, but despite her efforts to hold in her words, she shared, "Someone's recently been looking at your file."

Ariel's heart thumped hard against her ribs. "Someone's been in my file? Who?"

The social worker shrugged her slim shoulders. "I don't know. But if I were a rich man, I might look into the woman I was about to propose to...."

But if David had, he wouldn't have proposed. "No, it wasn't him." She hoped it was one of her sisters, that they were looking for her, as she was looking for them. But she knew what hope got a person—heart-wrenching disappointment. Still, she voiced the possibility to Margaret. "It could have been Irina or Elena. They could be looking for me."

And if they were, they would have already found her. But Margaret might not realize that. "Help me find them," Ariel implored the woman again.

Margaret shook her head. "If I got caught getting into their files…"

It would be her job. And Margaret still cared. Child Protective Services needed her. But so did Ariel.

"I *have* to find them."

"I remember every detail of that day I was put in

the system," Margaret said. "You weren't that young.
You probably remember more than you think."

Most times more than she wanted to. She remembered all the fear, all the pain, as she'd been
torn away from her mother. "How will remembering that day help me find my sisters?"

"You could start with your mother."

The killer had already found her. Through Ariel's
file? Was that who had looked inside? Ariel had to
find Elena and Irina before he did, before it was too
late, as she'd been for Haylee…and her mother.

The sound of her boot heels clicking against the
cement echoed throughout the parking garage and
inside his head. He narrowed his eyes as he watched
her walk toward her Jeep. She was the kind of
woman men watched, striking with her long red
hair and willowy body. The kind of woman who
could bewitch a man with her beauty, cast him so
completely under her spell that he'd forget his
purpose. She'd even tempted *him*.

But he wasn't like his ancestors. He was immune
to all witchcraft because he could be as strong as
they were, even stronger once they were all dead.
Because of that quest for power, he would *never*
forget his purpose.

She'd left the Jeep unlocked, making it so easy

for him to slip in the back. Before she even realized he was there, he could slit her throat. Just one quick swipe of the blade and it would be done. Too soon. Too easy. He needed more than that, needed to watch her suffer as his ancestors had suffered. As he suffered.

So today he let her pass in front of him. Her foot-steps slowed and she turned back, staring through the windshield right at him. Because of the tinted glass, she couldn't see him. But somehow she knew he was there.

Hatred clenched his hands into fists, but he re-strained himself, not reaching for the door handle. Not stepping out to face her. Finally she turned away and started walking again. And he let her go, get into her vehicle and drive away. This time.

He uncurled his fingers, then smoothed them out over the ancient leather-bound journal on his lap. Just touching it connected him to his roots. He opened it up and carefully flipped through the pages, the edges burned by flames and brittle with age. Reading it brought him so clearly back to his past, it was as if he lived it:

> *She* came to the house today. I have not
> seen such beauty but in a flower or the sky.
> I do not believe she's human. Mother said

she is a witch and sent us inside for our protection. With the door ajar, we could hear
them. Mother's voice, low and hostile, like
the dog is when we bother it when it's
feeding. Hers was musical, soft and mysteri-
ous. She warned Mother of a fire, sent from
the sky by lightning. Mother called her
warning a threat and a trick. She told her that
she is not easy to spook or fool. Yet when she
came inside, she was trembling with fear. I
wonder, does she fear the woman's words or
her beauty?

His hand shook with rage as he closed the journal.
This was how it had begun, so long ago, but there was
so much more not written by this female ancestor.
She had perished in that fire, burned alive. Only her
journal, left on the porch outside, had remained.

Her father, who had survived her as well as his
wife and other daughters, had avenged her death by
killing the first witch. He had written the rest, ex-
tolling how the witch's power had become his. As
soon as the witch had died at his hand, he'd begun
having visions, glimpses of the future, as she'd had.
With the death of each of her distant relatives he'd
tracked down, he'd gotten stronger. But he'd never
found the daughter…the one his son had let escape

that night with the charms, over three hundred and fifty years ago.

If not for the necessity to continue his line, he might have killed Thomas for his betrayal. But the girl had bewitched the boy with her beauty as well as her powers. To kill him for what he himself had succumbed to would have been hypocrisy. Eli McGregor had not been a hypocrite no matter what others who'd read the book believed. He had been a man with a mission. More than three centuries later, that mission would be carried out.

As soon as the old woman had given him the book, he had read it all. He knew every secret now, the other things his ancestor had admitted only in the pages of his private journal. Other descendants had considered the writings the ramblings of a madman. Not him. Slowly the power Eli had discovered was becoming his. He set the journal on the passenger seat, where it dislodged the file already lying there. Photocopies slid out, the letterhead bearing the name and address of Child Protective Services for the city of Barrett, Michigan.

The old woman had given him the book, but she'd kept some other things from him. Important things. But it didn't matter now. He'd found most of her secrets, and if there was anything else he needed to know, he would learn that, too. But not

when his female ancestor had learned so long ago—
too late. Not until the original owner of the journal
was caught in a burning house had the little girl
finally realized her mother was right. The Durikken
woman was a witch.

He was counting on Ariel using her powers to
lead him to the others. And their charms. Then he
could kill her, and once he had the charms in his
possession, he would kill her sisters, too.

Chapter 4

Armaya, Gypsy for *curse*. The name ringing in her ears, Ariel had pulled up maps of Michigan on the computer and she'd found the town, the tiniest dot a few hours north of Barrett. As Margaret had said, Ariel had not been that young when she'd been taken away from her mom and separated from her sisters. She could remember that day, so she should be able to remember some other things about that time of her life. But even though she'd tried, the only thing that had come to her was *Armaya*.

Now she was going to it, steering her Jeep up the highway to that dot, which had only appeared on old maps, more like a smudge than a designated town. Was it still there? She hadn't found it on any current maps, but that didn't matter. She had to at least look for it.

She glanced down at the ring gleaming on her hand, the diamond reflecting prisms of light onto the headliner. She had to go back to go forward. Until she knew where her sisters were and that they were safe, she wouldn't be able to think about *her* future. They probably wouldn't appreciate her disrupting their lives and reminding them of their pasts, but she'd risk their anger to protect them. She'd risk more pain and rejection, too. She had to…for her sisters.

Cold coffee churned in her stomach. The paper cup sat askew in the beverage holder; the drips oozing under the lid and down the side looked more like sludge than coffee. But she couldn't blame the caffeine for her nausea. Guilt nagged at her. Since his proposal, she'd been avoiding David, offering excuses of being too busy to meet him for lunch or dinner, and that had been when she'd answered his calls. Most of the time she'd let her cell ring into voice mail, her guilt increasing as she'd replayed his messages and heard the concern resonate in his deep voice.

But she wasn't really avoiding *him,* she was avoiding the *truth.* False truths and honest lies.

Would he accept the Gypsy proverb? She doubted it. He hadn't achieved all his success with dumb luck. The man was too smart. He would know she'd kept her secret to protect herself, not him.

Sighing, she glanced into the rearview mirror and caught a familiar sight—a black van—passing a semi and slipping behind the SUV tailing Ariel. The SUV didn't bother her; it had just entered the expressway on the last on-ramp. But that van had been somewhere behind her since Barrett. She wasn't certain, but it could be the one she'd noticed a couple of days ago in the parking garage of social services.

Usually the light and mist distracted her from details such as other vehicles, but like heat rising off the asphalt, the orange glow shimmered only on the road ahead as if leading her toward Armaya. The rearview mirror kept drawing Ariel's attention from the light. Something about the van—maybe that the windows were tinted so dark that it looked as if there was no driver—quickened her pulse and added to her uneasiness.

Noting the exit for gas and food, she jerked the wheel, cutting in front of a minivan to maneuver her Jeep onto the off-ramp. The driver blared her horn, and Ariel lifted her hand in an apologetic wave. Then the horn blared again as a black van swerved onto the exit, too. Ariel's heart kicked hard in her chest. Not good. This was not good. Why was someone following her?

The coffee churned in her stomach again. She would have been the easiest to find, staying in Barrett and keeping her name. Had her mother's killer found her already? Or maybe it was as she'd hoped—maybe one of her sisters was looking for her. She might never know if she kept running.

She reached toward the passenger seat, where her purse sat. By the time she'd pulled up near a pump at the station, she had extracted a can of pepper spray from the leather bag. For a second she wished it were a gun, but as a teacher, she would have never felt comfortable carrying one. The pepper spray was dangerous enough that she'd always locked up her purse so the kids wouldn't get ahold of it. But she didn't have to worry about the children anymore, not unless she let David manipulate the school board into requesting her reinstatement. She wouldn't ask him to intercede on her behalf, though. Since seeing her mother's ghost, she wasn't ready to go back. If she didn't find out who was following her, she might never have the opportunity.

She clutched the canister tightly in one hand as she opened the door of the Jeep with the other. The mingled odors of gasoline and oil hung heavily on the air, thicker than the mist. After walking past the pumps, she rounded the corner of the painted white brick station, hoping that anyone watching her would think she was heading to the restrooms. A glance over her shoulder confirmed that the van had pulled into the parking lot, too, near the air pumps on the other side.

Ariel circled around the back of the building, where most of the paint had peeled from the old red bricks. She skirted the garbage-reeking Dumpsters, where flies buzzed, then edged toward the corner. Her heart thumped hard, the beat in her chest echoing in her palm as she tightly clutched the canister. What protection would the pepper spray be against a knife or a gun? Enough if she acted quickly?

She searched her brain for the knowledge garnered from the self-defense course she'd taken during college. But all she remembered was the advice to run as far and as fast from potential danger as possible, shrieking loudly.

Even knowing the advice she should be taking, she hunched over, then slipped around the corner, setting her feet softly and carefully on the sidewalk hugging the building so no loose gravel crunched beneath the heels of her boots. Slinking down low, she edged up the side of the black van until she neared the driver's door. The sunlight reflected off only a sliver of glass above the door, as the window was down. Drawing in a quick, ragged breath, she stood and pointed the spray can into the open window. "Who the hell are—"

The dark eyes of the driver widened with surprise, followed by a darker shadow of guilt, then a flash of pride. "You caught me," David said, a slight grin lifting his mouth.

Hands shaking, she lowered the can so she wouldn't inadvertently spray him even though she was tempted. He almost deserved it for the scare he'd given her. Anger sharpened her voice as she asked, "Why were you following me?"

"I was worried about you," he admitted, opening the van door to step out beside her. "You've been acting so strangely."

Ever since the night her mother's ghost had appeared. Despite the warm sweater she wore over her blouse, she shivered, then insisted, "I wasn't running away again."

His brown eyes narrowed with doubt as his voice softened with concern. "I was worried that you might. That maybe I put too much pressure on you with my proposal."

She couldn't deny that he had, but the pressure was on her to be honest, to put herself out there for the man she loved. Maybe taking him to Armaya was the first step; it might be easier to show than tell. That was the advice she'd always given her shy students to participate in class.

"This trip has nothing to do with us." Not really, not until now. "I'm trying to find someone."

"Let me help you, Ariel. Who are you looking for?" David asked.

She drew in a quick breath, but it didn't ease the ache in her chest. "My mother."

She was part of the reason for Ariel's return to Armaya. Ariel needed to find out how her mom had died, and if it was, as she suspected, murder, to make certain that the killer was brought to justice. Hopefully he had already been caught and there was no threat to her or her sisters. But her mother's image burned in Ariel's mind, her arms flailing, her mouth open as if screaming or shouting a warning.

"You told me you were a foster child."

She nodded. "That's true, but I wasn't an orphan." Then. But she'd let him believe she was so that she didn't have to answer questions about her family, not because she was ashamed of them but because it hurt too much to explain that they'd never looked for her. All they had had to do to find her was open the Barrett phone book. "I was put into foster care after I was taken away from my mom and split up from my sisters."

"Sisters?" Shock cracked his deep voice. "You have sisters?"

"Yes. One older. One younger." Women she wouldn't know if she passed them on the street. Strangers.

"Do you know where they are?" he asked.

She shook her head. "No, but I remember where we lived when social services took us away from my mom. A little town just north of here—if it's still there."

His arms closed around her, pulling her close, offering that comfort he always instinctively knew she needed. His heart beat sure and steady beneath her cheek. More than the diamond on her finger, David was her rock. "I'll go with you," he said.

She didn't want to lose him. Fighting against the urge to melt in his arms, she pulled back. She'd already shocked him with what she'd revealed; she could tell by how dark his eyes were, how taut his jaw was as she glanced up at him. "Maybe it's better that I go alone."

"Ariel, let me in…."

If she was ever going to accept his proposal, she had to. She drew in a deep breath, then nodded. "All right."

But even as she agreed, she worried that once he learned the truth, she'd lose him.

* * *

"Why didn't you ever tell me about your past before?" David asked as he closed his laptop and tossed it into the back of the van.

On the passenger side she settled against the contoured leather bench seat, the fabric soft and supple, unlike the cracked vinyl of the Jeep's driver's seat. But she stared longingly at her Cherokee as they left it in the carpool lot next to the gas station and headed back onto the freeway.

"It's not easy to talk about," she answered truthfully. Despite what she'd told him—mostly just her mother's and sisters' names—she'd left so much unsaid.

He reached across the width of the seat, covering her hand with his. "It must have been traumatic."

Being torn away from people who actually understood and accepted her? She closed her eyes as the remembered despair pressed down on her chest, stealing her breath away. His fingers tightened around her hand, offering a comforting squeeze.

Why didn't she feel comforted? Because his touch invoked memories of passion, images flickering behind her lids of the two of them entwined in bed? His hands moving over her naked skin, stroking her breasts, her thighs. Her pulse quickened but with more than sexual awareness. She felt an uneasiness, like when she'd noticed the van following her. Maybe it wasn't fear of David's rejection that had compelled her to keep her past secret. Maybe she feared David. He was a powerful man, used to getting what he wanted. He wanted her. Because he loved her, as he claimed?

Ariel didn't trust love. After the rejections she'd suffered, she didn't trust anyone or anything. Not even David. Maybe most especially David, since her feelings made her the most vulnerable to him.

"Ariel, are you okay?" he asked.

"Scared," she admitted, being more honest with him than she'd ever been.

"Don't be. I'm here for you."

Now.

"I'll always be here for you."

How had he spoken to her unexpressed thought? Luck, deep knowledge of her…or something else?

She opened her eyes, to the thick smoke, to the orange glow. Was her mother back to warn her away from or to lead her toward Armaya? Gypsy for *curse,* it had probably been named for the Durikken curse, the special abilities that people mistrusted and mistook for witchcraft. But then, they really hadn't been mistaken. Ariel's ancestors had been witches. So was she.

She hoped the little town held the information

she needed to find and warn her sisters. She wasn't just worried about them, though. She was worried about David, too, about what she'd told him. Not enough but maybe too much. She tugged her hand free of his and clenched it into a fist in her lap. Trying to keep her past secret would alienate him, but telling him everything...

Damn her inability to trust.

"This could be a dead end," David warned, his deep voice directed toward the windshield as he concentrated on the road. He'd turned off the highway a while back. "Are you prepared for that?"

She peered through the smoke to the image of her mother, her eyes burning with anguish, her mouth open as she tried to speak. Or scream? Ariel resisted the urge to shudder and assured him, "I'm prepared for anything."

"I can vouch for that," David said with a chuckle. "I never knew you carried mace."

"Pepper spray."

"I guess that might not have blinded me then," he said ruefully.

She wasn't about to apologize for protecting herself. "So you were following me because you were worried about me?" She shouldn't doubt that he cared about her; he'd proven it again and again.

"Yes, I was worried," he admitted again. "You

were avoiding my calls, cutting yourself off from everyone—"

"So you thought I was going to run."

He sighed. "I didn't know what you were going to do."

"I ran *once*," she defended herself. At least it was once that he knew of; the other times she'd run away from foster homes before they could get rid of her by either sending her to another or locking her up in a psychiatric hospital.

"When you were overwhelmed," David agreed. Speaking of Haylee or to her thoughts again?

"Yes…"

"I thought I had overwhelmed you again with my proposal," he explained.

"It was a surprise," she said, glancing down at the diamond, aglow with reflections of the orange light.

"I'm not rushing you," he insisted. "Take all the time you need to decide."

She wasn't taking the time to make her decision; she was using it to avoid telling him the truth. She couldn't give him an answer until she did. But first she had a question of her own. "So how long have you been following me?"

"From your house."

"What about yesterday?" Had that been his van at Child Protective Services? She hadn't studied it long enough to determine the make or model; those weren't things she'd know anyway. But it had been black like his, and she'd suspected someone had been inside, hidden behind the dark tinted windows, watching her. She shivered again, as she'd done yesterday in the cold, damp garage.

He shook his head, but sunglasses concealed his eyes and whatever else he might be hiding from her. Once again she had a feeling she wasn't the only one keeping secrets.

"I'm not stalking you," he vowed. "I was driving up to your house, intending to talk to you, when you pulled out of the driveway. I didn't consciously decide to follow you, but…"

"You did," she pointed out. "I didn't even know you had a van."

He shrugged, his broad shoulders rippling beneath his leather jacket. "It belongs to the company, one of the fleet."

But devoid of logo or brand. Why had he used it instead of his more luxurious Cadillac Escalade? So she wouldn't recognize him? Was that the action of a man worried she was running away or a man wanting to follow her to know where she was going?

Her stomach churned with the doubts. She should accept him at his word. He wasn't a stalker. He was the man who loved her.

"Do you recognize it?" David asked.

Love and concern? Probably not, she'd seen so little of it in her life. "What?"

"The town. We're here."

She glanced out the window. The assorted collection of frame and brick buildings sitting at the curb of cobblestone streets didn't look much different from a dozen other small towns they'd passed through since he'd pulled off the highway. "No, I don't."

"Well, the Cooper listed in the Armaya property tax records doesn't live in town." That was what he'd pulled up on his laptop—tax records as well as more up-to-date maps. "We have a few miles to go yet."

But those few miles of woods and fields didn't do anything to jar Ariel's memory. Whatever hope she had harbored dimmed, just like the orange glow that had led her north. Her mother was gone. "It doesn't matter. They're not here."

She and her sisters had been taken away from this little town two decades ago. She wouldn't find them in Armaya. The only thing she might find was her mother's body.

"Probably not," David agreed. "But someone in town might remember you and your sisters, might have kept track of the three of you."

That was something else she was afraid of—that someone already knew where her sisters were.

"Why now, Ariel?" David asked as he turned toward her. The dark glasses concealed his eyes, so she didn't know if curiosity or something else motivated his question.

"What do you mean?" She hated the suspicion coloring her perception of the man she loved. He'd never been anything but sweet and generous. Why did she doubt his motives? Because of the appearance of her mother's ghost? Or was she using her mother to justify doubts she already harbored and had ignored until now?

"Why are you looking for your mom and sisters now?" he persisted.

She'd shared as much with him as she dared for the moment. If she told him the rest—about her special ability—he'd think she was crazy, as Margaret had and all those people before her.

"I just need to find them."

"Did losing Haylee bring all that back for you, losing them?" he asked, his voice even deeper with concern.

Ariel expelled a little sigh. She was being ridiculous. "I really can't explain."

Because she'd have to tell him that she hadn't really lost Haylee. She wasn't sure why the little girl hadn't left her yet; maybe she knew Ariel needed her as an anchor to hold on to during turmoil. But

Haylee was in a better place, and every time she appeared to Ariel she seemed at peace.

Unlike Ariel's mother, who was tortured even in death. *Oh, Mama…*

Ariel hoped to find her grave here in Armaya, assuming her body had been found. Just in case, she'd brought a spray of brown-eyed Susans, which she'd always picked for her mother whenever they'd stayed in Armaya. Regret pulled at her heart; she'd left them back in the Jeep.

"Don't worry," David assured Ariel. "We'll find your family, wherever they are." He pulled the van down a dirt road, gravel spewing from the tires as the vehicle bounced over ruts.

Maybe it was the cold air blowing from the vents, but a chill chased across Ariel's skin. This was it. Where that truck camper had been parked that day. In a cornfield behind the old frame farmhouse that barely stood on a broken-down stone foundation.

"Here," she said, her voice lifting with excitement. "Turn here."

"You recognize it?" David asked as if he doubted her twenty-year-old memories. "But it doesn't look like anyone lives here."

It looked condemned, but that was how Ariel remembered it looking all those years ago. And an old man had lived in the house—her grandfather. Papa

Cooper. He'd been too stubborn to do anything to keep up the house and property. *They would only raise my taxes if I did.* That was one of her only memories of the gnarled old man. He couldn't be alive anymore. He'd been so old back then, so frightening, like a skeleton that moved and talked, far scarier than any of the ghosts she'd seen.

But she, her mother and sisters hadn't stayed long or all that often at the farm, only coming by for fleeting visits. For parties. Another memory flashed through Ariel's mind: picnic tables strewn about the overgrown yard, music playing, people dancing. Most of the people had probably been neighbors or friends, but Ariel remembered a couple of women who had looked like her mother. Her aunts. Why had neither of them taken Ariel and her sisters? Why had no one tried to keep them together?

She wouldn't know any answers unless she asked the questions. There had to be someone here who could tell her what she needed to know, who could help her find her mother.

On the edge of the two-track drive, flowers bloomed among the overgrown weeds, their brown faces tilting toward the sun as their golden petals glowed like its rays. Needing comfort, she reached for her bracelet, to the worn pewter charm dangling from it. Despite the cool air in the van, the metal was warm, and as she stroked the charm, the light appeared, burning through the overcast clouds, shimmering in the mist that suddenly blanketed the old farm.

"Looks deserted," David commented, gesturing toward the bare boards of the old farmhouse, the weather having stripped whatever color paint from it long ago.

Ariel would argue with him, but she couldn't explain that the place was far from deserted. Spirits remained. She had yet to see them, but the mist and light assured her of their presence. Maybe this was where her mother's life had ended.

"There's a car parked by the barn. It looks like it runs. Someone must be here," David observed, as he turned off the engine. He turned toward her, his brown eyes bright with excitement.

She wished she could summon some excitement, too, but she'd finally heeded his earlier cautions not to get her hopes up. If only spirits lived here, they wouldn't be able to help her. She wouldn't *hear* what they tried to tell her.

When David exited the car, she didn't wait for him to open her door as he always did. She threw it open and climbed out, her legs tingling from the long ride. Then she glanced toward the house again.

A shadow emerged from under the sagging roof.

A dark-haired woman with large, dark eyes stared out at her. Ariel started, for a moment thinking it was again the vision of her mother. But, no, this woman was older, her features a little rougher. One of Ariel's aunts.

David took her hand. "Let's go knock, see if anyone's home," he said, looking straight at the house, at the woman on the porch. But he didn't see her. Ariel realized she wasn't real. Not anymore.

Ariel's breath shuddered out.

"Nervous?" David asked. "Don't worry. I'm here. I'm with you."

And so was someone else…in spirit. Was the body here, too? She didn't have to wait long to find out. As they walked across the porch, the front door creaked open. Even in the dim interior lighting, Ariel glimpsed the dangling legs.

David gasped. "Oh, my God!"

He rushed forward, shouldering open the door the rest of the way as he reached toward the woman. But Ariel caught his arm, her fingers clutching at his sleeve.

"No, it's too late." Even without seeing the woman's blank stare from a stiff face drained of color, Ariel would have known she was already dead. Her ghost hovered near her body, her mouth open as she tried to communicate. But Ariel would

never know what the woman might have been able
to tell her about her mother or her sisters.

"Oh, my God," David said again, staring up at the
corpse. "Ariel, are you all right?"

No. Fear pressed hard against her heart, slowing
its beat. As David had warned her earlier, this had
turned out to be a dead end. For this poor woman.

And for Ariel.

Chapter 5

Ariel leaned against the porch railing, testing the rotted wood as she watched the van back down the driveway toward the gravel road. David searched for a cell signal. Thinking Armaya might not have a satellite, he'd wanted her to go with him to find the police station. But she'd pleaded the need for air so she could stay behind.

She'd promised she wouldn't leave the porch. But as soon as the dust kicked up from behind the van's tires, she pushed open the door to the house and slipped around the woman's dangling body. Maybe Ariel was more like her mother than she thought, because with each lie she told, the next one came more easily.

But she'd come to Armaya to look for information that would help locate her sisters; she wasn't going to leave without at least trying. Better to search the house with David gone. He wouldn't understand how finding this woman dead increased her urgency instead of distracting her from her goal, not unless she told him everything—and she wasn't ready to do that yet.

She glanced up at the body hanging from one of the open rafters in the old country kitchen. From her approximate age and Gypsy appearance, the woman was likely her aunt, probably an older sister to her mother. Her ghost hadn't sought out Ariel. Ariel had had to come to her. Why? Was there something in the house that would lead her to her mother's body, or her sisters?

She wished she had remembered the town before, when she was eighteen and desperate to find her family. But she'd been so scared that they wouldn't want to see her she'd probably mentally blocked out the name of the town then. She'd only remembered now because she thought her sisters were in danger.

As she headed toward the back of the house, worn pine floorboards creaking beneath her feet, she glanced over her shoulder at the body again. She was *certain* her sisters were in danger.

Smoke poured into the low-ceilinged hall and orange light glimmered from under the door of a room at the end. Hand trembling, Ariel turned the knob and let herself inside. Dust motes danced on the afternoon sunshine streaking through a dirty window, and the scent of sandalwood and lavender hung heavily in the air. "Mama?"

Even though she couldn't hear her, her mother's ghost might still lead her to what Ariel needed. But someone had beaten her to the back room. Drawers stood open, pulled from a desk in a corner of the room. Boxes had been overturned, the contents spilled across the scarred wood floor.

Ariel dropped to her knees and delved trembling hands into the papers, desperate to find anything that might help locate her sisters. But there was nothing left to be found. Had *he* found where they were?

The barest brush against her shoulder startled her. But when she whirled around, no one stood behind her. The smoke thickened, then her mother appeared, her ghost glowing as if afire, her eyes wide with pain and fear. Her mouth moving.

"I can't hear you, Mama," Ariel said as she blinked back tears. Her ability to *see* ghosts couldn't help her. Her mother couldn't help her.

Only Ariel could help Ariel. She glanced down at a small square of glossy cardboard on the floor. A postcard. She picked it up and flipped it over. Across the back was scrawled a message, something innocuous. The words didn't matter; the symbols below her mother's signature did. A moon, a star and a sun.

The charms.

She reached for the pewter sun dangling against her wrist, rubbing the warm metal between her fingertips. "It's supposed to keep me safe," she remembered. "God, I hope Elena and Irina still have theirs."

But would the little charms be enough to protect them from a killer? Staring into her mother's terrified face, she doubted it. Then Mama's ghost pointed toward the card, so Ariel glanced down at it again, noticing the circle drawn around those symbols.

Did they need to be together, all three charms, to protect them?

"I'll find them," she promised Mama as she slipped the postcard into her pocket.

Sirens wailed in the distance, and outside the single-paned window, tires crunched over gravel. The black van cast a shadow into the room as the smoke and light receded. Despite David's return, she felt alone. Vulnerable. She needed her sisters, not just to keep them alive but to stay alive herself.

* * *

"Turn in here," Ariel said, reaching over to grasp David's arm, her trembling fingers clutching at his leather sleeve.

He obliged, steering the van through the opening in the cobblestone wall surrounding Armaya Cemetery. "What do you want in here?"

Not more ghosts. She already saw too many of them. She was hoping instead to find answers. "I need to see my family plot, David." Her breath caught, then escaped in a ragged sigh. "I need to see if my mother's…"

Buried.

He shut off the ignition and clasped his hand over hers. "She's not dead, Ariel. When I used the laptop back at the car park, I looked for a death certificate for her. There wasn't one. Unless she got married and changed her name."

Irony tugged Ariel's lips into a smile. "Oh, I doubt my mother ever got married." Since she hadn't wed any of the fathers of her children, she wasn't likely to have ever become a bride. And now she would never have the chance. Ariel's mouth pulled down, and she bit her bottom lip to still its faint tremble.

"You haven't seen her in a long time," David said.

But he was wrong. Ariel saw her now, in the smoke

and the orange light that glowed through the thick branches of the oak under which the woman hovered.

"From what the sheriff's deputy said, *no one's* seen your mother in Armaya in a long time," David continued. "She's not here, Ariel."

Wrong again. Just as the deputy had been wrong when he'd said her aunt's death was most likely a suicide. Ariel hadn't corrected him, knowing that without proof the deputy and David would have thought her crazy. They didn't realize hanging was one way witches had been killed. Hanged. Burned at the stake.

Fear chilled her, raising goose bumps on her skin and lifting the fine hair on her nape. She knew what it all meant. Someone had started the witch hunt again.

"Ariel, are you all right?"

She only nodded, not trusting herself to speak. When his arms closed around her, she pressed her cheek against his chest, where his heart beat sure and steady. But she didn't want to use David, as her mother had used rich men, to keep her safe. Ariel was stronger than that; she was stronger than her mother had been. And when she found her sisters and their charms, she would be even stronger.

"I'm fine," she assured him, pulling from his embrace.

David stared at her for a moment, as if gauging her truthfulness, before he started the van back up.

"Maybe we should talk to the caretaker," he said, slowing to a stop just inside the cobblestone wall, "and make arrangements for your aunt."

"Like you did for Haylee."

A muscle moved in his jaw. "How'd you find that out?"

His generosity—and his desire to keep it anonymous, was what had first attracted Ariel to David. That and his golden hair and deep brown eyes. Her heart fluttered a bit, lighter than it had been since they'd found her aunt.

"Margaret told me," she admitted.

"The social worker? You've seen her?"

Ariel narrowed her eyes, studying his profile. Was he really surprised or feigning it so that she wouldn't suspect it had been his van in the parking garage the day she'd gone to Margaret's office? Mistrust pressed against her heart, weighing it down again.

"I talked to her," she said. "Tried to get her to give me information that would help me find my sisters."

"She wouldn't help?"

Ariel shook her head. "She couldn't, not without risking her job. I shouldn't have asked."

"Not her, Ariel. You should have asked *me*. I can help you. I can pull up all kinds of stuff on the computer." She suspected he was talking about more than Internet search engines. Some of the news articles about him that he hated so much claimed that he'd been quite the hacker when he was younger, that even now the FBI and CIA often sought his advice. He'd denied the claims as exaggeration, but she didn't doubt his expertise. Her heart sinking even more, she realized it was only a matter of time before he learned everything about her.

She knew he hadn't checked her out as Margaret had suspected, or she wouldn't be wearing his ring. Why hadn't he? Guilt churned in her stomach when she realized it was because he trusted her.

She couldn't worry herself now. Finding her sisters was more important. "You can get into sealed adoption records?"

His broad shoulders lifted in a shrug. "I can try."

He would break laws for her, and she couldn't even be completely honest with him. "David…"

"What, honey?"

"Thank you." She couldn't say anything more. "Don't worry about the arrangements, though. The deputy said someone would take care of things for Marie Cooper." The woman who'd been hanged.

"But he wouldn't tell you who."

Because he hadn't completely believed her. He didn't remember Myra Cooper having children; of course she'd been young when she'd left Armaya. He might have told David about any next of kin Marie had if David had asked, but he'd been curiously withdrawn back at the farmhouse. Ariel pushed aside her frustration. She'd find out if there were any other Coopers left in Armaya when she attended her aunt's funeral.

"Do you want to stop in town?" David asked as he steered the van down the cobblestone street running through the little village of Armaya.

Ariel considered it. But she suspected the townspeople might be less open with her than the deputy had been. Or worse, they might be more open, telling things to David that she needed to tell him herself.

She would do that. Soon. Then she would come back to Armaya. Alone.

He couldn't breathe again. The smoke was too thick, surrounding him. His eyes burned, nearly blinding him. But still he could see them with the hoods covering their hair and most of their faces except for their smiling mouths, their lips red and rounded as they laughed. At him.

This was no dream. He was wide-awake, sitting at his desk, the glowing banker's lamp dispelling the darkness of the room but not of that inside his soul. The vision taunted him, forever teasing at his

consciousness, warning him of what was to come
if he took no action, what still might come even
though he had.

He'd killed two women but only one witch. With
her death, by fire, her memories had become his,
living as vividly in his mind as his own. He'd seen
her visions. The same had happened for his
ancestor, the man whose handwritten words called
from the open pages of the journal, reminding him
of his purpose.

The second woman had sworn she had no special
abilities, that not all Durikken women were witches.
Perhaps that was why she hadn't run like her
sister—because she'd thought she was safe. But he
hadn't believed her...until he'd hanged her. Then,
instead of feeling more powerful, he'd felt less. He
wasn't a killer, just taking lives for sport. He had a
mission, as he'd told those he recruited, those over
whom he had power. He could make *them* do
whatever he wanted. He could probably make them
do the killing if there came a time when he couldn't.

A flash of pride in his brilliance warmed the
coldness of his heart. He'd formed an alliance to
combat witchcraft. He had found others who
abhorred it, who'd been bilked by fortunetellers or
psychics and wanted revenge. He'd manipulated
them to take up his agenda as theirs.

Despite what the doctors told him, he was getting stronger. Not weaker. But in his head, the women's laughter echoed. He might have power over his followers but not over them, not the witches. He wouldn't have power over them until they were all dead and he had the charms back where they belonged.

In his possession.

Ariel jerked awake, blinking to clear the mist from her vision. But it remained, thick like smoke and scented with sandalwood and lavender instead of burning wood.

"Mama…"

She squinted against the orange glow but could make out no image of her mother. Still, she knew she was there or somewhere close. "I will find my sisters," she vowed again.

Since she hadn't *seen* them yet, they had to be alive. Didn't they? If Ariel could see the ghosts of strangers, certainly she'd see her sisters once they passed. Yet for the strangers, she happened upon them at hospitals or cemeteries. They didn't seek her out. After all these years, her sisters were strangers to her. Since they hadn't sought her while they were alive, why would they after death?

As the light faded, she opened her eyes wider.

She lay in the middle of a king-size bed with a black leather headboard and black satin sheets. A chandelier hung above her, glittering in the faint light seeping beneath the door from the hall. Ariel flung back the sheets, finding herself fully clothed in her jeans and long-sleeved peasant blouse. Her sweater lay over a chair beside the bed.

David's bed. She'd only ever lain in it naked and never alone. Face flushing at hot memories, she reached up to brush her tangled hair back from her face, wincing as something sharp scraped her cheek. Glancing down, she saw that the diamond ring had twisted on her finger. A droplet of blood clung to the sharp stone before falling into her palm. *Her* blood, the sight of which usually made her woozy. Maybe because it always felt prophetic…that her blood would be shed someday.

Even though she'd occasionally tried to convince herself that the curse was a fairy tale, she'd never really accepted her own assurances. All she'd had to do was see the mist, the light and someone's ghost and she'd known that her mother had spoken the truth.

Too anxious to be woozy, she wiped the blood on her jeans and opened the door to the hall. Along the sides of an Oriental runner, polished mahogany flooring gleamed in the light cast by several mini chandeliers hanging from the high ceiling. Ariel never felt entirely comfortable in David's penthouse due to its size and elegance; it was more showplace than home. Today she was even more uneasy, like someone locked in a museum after closing. Her footsteps echoed eerily in the cavernous space. She felt too alone, too vulnerable.

Mist swirled down the wide corridor, then thickened to smoke. "Mama?" she whispered, but no ghost appeared. Was she losing her ability somehow?

When she was younger, when foster families had rejected her over her curse, she'd hated it and tried to no avail to blind herself to the light and the mist. But without her ability, she was denying who she was. Maybe not being a witch would save her life, but what kind of life would it be if she couldn't do what she'd always done? If she lost such an important part of her identity?

As much as it sometimes overwhelmed her, the way it had when she'd first seen Haylee's ghost and her mother's, she couldn't imagine being without it. She couldn't imagine losing that connection to another world. And after the weeks she'd been away, she couldn't imagine her life without David. She called out his name, her voice echoing. "David? Where are you?"

She poked her head into open doors, finding only

empty guest rooms. He was probably downstairs, either in the living room or the offices of his business. He also had a study somewhere on this floor. She kept checking rooms until she came to a closed door. Her fingers gripped the knob, turning it. The door rattled in the jamb but didn't open. "David?" She rapped her knuckles against the mahogany two-panel door. "David?"

No one answered from within. She turned away, heading for the stairs. Suddenly the door rattled again as someone unlocked it, then David stepped out. She only caught a glimpse of green light glowing against dark wood before he pulled the door closed behind him.

"Ariel, are you all right?" he asked, taking her in his arms.

Her pulse leaped. "No."

"Shh," he murmured into her hair as he pulled her closer. "It's all right. I'm here."

"Why'd you lock the door?" she asked, mistrust churning her stomach. Would she ever be able to freely give her trust, her love?

He shrugged, his broad shoulders rippling beneath the black silk shirt he wore. "Habit. I've got business stuff in there, can't have just anyone stumbling on it."

Her lips tipped into a smile, reassured by his reasonable explanation. "Am I just anyone?"

He drew in a breath. "You're *everything,* Ariel."

Warmth spread through her chest. She couldn't lose him. She might not ever be able to completely trust someone, but her love for David was much stronger than her doubts about him. "David…"

Strong fingers tipped up her chin, then slid across her cheek. He held his hand in front of him, a drop of blood smeared across it. "You're bleeding! What happened? What hurt you?"

She shrugged, dismissing the wound. "It's nothing. Just a scratch. I caught myself with the ring."

"Damn," he breathed, his brown eyes darkening. "Ariel—"

She reached up and pressed her fingers against his lips. "Don't worry. I'm fine." Now. In his arms.

Not that she felt safe in his embrace. She felt everything else. Passion. Heat. Most importantly she felt alive. With all the death she'd seen over the years, nothing meant more to her than life. And David.

She gazed up at him, hypnotized by the way the light made his hair shine, by the strength of his jaw, the small dimple in his chin, the fullness of his lips despite the masculinity of them, of him. She'd never known more man than David Koster.

Even though she'd done her share of dating over the years, she'd never fallen so hard so fast for anyone before. She skimmed her fingertips back and forth across his lips as his breath sighed out against her skin. "David…"

His arms tightened around her. "I love the way you say my name. I love you."

She had to tell him the truth now, before he found out on his own. "David…"

He shuddered at her touch. Then he tipped up her chin, his mouth descending on hers in an all-consuming kiss. His lips pressed hers apart, his tongue sweeping possessively against hers.

He pulled away, panting for breath. "Ariel, it's late."

Night had fallen by the time they'd driven back from Armaya. She'd insisted on picking up her Jeep from the car park and driving it home, but she'd been exhausted by the time they'd gotten back to Barrett. Too tired for the conversation she needed to have with David. Even though she'd followed him to the penthouse intent on telling him everything, she'd taken him up on his suggestion of resting for a while.

"You've been through a lot the last few weeks. You really should go back to bed," he said, more as if to convince himself than her.

"So take me," she told him as she linked her arms behind his neck. Guilt nipped at her as she inwardly admitted to stalling again. But she wasn't using David, as her mother had used men for money and protection. She loved him. Her heart clenched. She loved him too much.

A grin kicked up the corners of his mouth. "You're asking for it…."

His love. His forgiveness when he learned what she'd kept from him. She intended to ask for those, beg if she needed to, but she'd deal with that later. Right now she wanted David.

Chapter 6

David's dark eyes flaring with passion, he swung her up in his arms. Excitement burned hot in her veins and quivered in her stomach. She bounced against his chest as he strode for the bedroom, shouldering through the partially open door to playfully toss her down on the rumpled satin sheets.

"Last chance," he warned her. "If you don't want this, you better tell me to leave now."

She propped herself up on her elbows, causing the peasant blouse to slip from her shoulders. "I want *you,*" she insisted.

Heat flared in his dark eyes. "God, you are so

damned beautiful." He leaned over her, pressing a kiss to her bare shoulder. "You're bewitching."

If he only knew…

He blew out a ragged sigh, his breath caressing her skin and eliciting an involuntary shiver from her. "Ariel, after what you've just been through, finding your aunt—"

"I need you," she interrupted. "More now than ever. I need to feel alive." After seeing so much death.

She reached out, fumbling with the buttons on his silk shirt. Despite her trembling fingers, the material parted, revealing his broad chest. Moonlight streaked into the room through the slatted blinds, glancing off the sculpted muscles beneath satin skin.

She sat up more, sliding her mouth over his chest until she touched his heart. It throbbed beneath her lips, its beat fast and hard. He wanted her but he didn't reach for her. His arms were stiff at his sides, his jaw clenched.

"Such control," she murmured in awe. She lost hers anytime he touched her. She wanted to lose control, wanted to lose all sense of reality, because her reality made no sense. She reached for the slightly frayed hem of her blouse. Bypassing the lacing holding the front together, she pulled it over her head, revealing her beige demibra and bare skin.

He drew in an audible breath. "Ariel…"

"Touch me, David," she urged him, grabbing his hand to lay across her breast.

A grin tipped up the corners of his mouth. "I'll touch you," he promised, sensual intent heating his dark eyes. With just the slightest movement, he unhooked the clasp between her breasts. They spilled out of the cups, into his hands.

She moaned as he gently stroked her skin, tracing her curves with just the soft touch of his fingertips. Then his touch roughened, his thumbs pressing against her nipples, stroking them hard. Ariel arched her back as a cry tore from her lips. "David!"

"You want me to touch you," he reminded her. He slid his hands over her stomach, his fingers deftly unsnapping her jeans. Then in one swift motion he stood up and pulled them down her legs, nearly dragging her off the foot of the bed along with the denim.

As her bare back slid across the satin sheets, she shivered at the delicious sensation. Until that moment, she'd never really understood the appeal of the fabric. To her, it had always seemed cold. But with the fever raging to life inside her, she was anything but cold.

David must have thought she was, because he folded a sheet across her. Before she could protest, he was moving the fabric, stroking the satin across her bare skin, back and forth over the hard tips of her breasts. She moaned and shifted against the sheets, needing more. Answering her unspoken desire, he leaned over, closing his mouth over the sheet and her breast, suckling her nipple through the silky fabric.

Ariel's stomach quivered with each pull of his mouth on her skin, each nip of his teeth, gentled by the sheet. "David…"

He moved his hands, gliding them down the satin sheet, over her legs until he tilted her knees apart. Then he stroked the satin across her mound, back and forth.

Ariel gritted her teeth as the friction teased, but a moan slipped out. "David…"

He stared down at her, his dark eyes burning with desire. "What do you want, Ariel?" He slipped a finger, sheathed in satin, inside her.

Her muscles convulsed and she shuddered. "David, I want you. I need you!"

"You have me, Ariel," he insisted, but he kept teasing her, using the satin to stroke her skin and stoke her passion higher.

She moaned and thrashed her head against the pillows, totally at the mercy of his sensual torture. Then he pulled the sheet aside, cool air feathering across her skin. Nothing separated his mouth from her as his lips tortured her as the satin had, moving over her breasts and down between her legs. She sobbed as sensations rippled through her, rendering her mindless with ecstasy.

When she thought she could take no more, he stepped back, dropped his jeans and rolled on protection. Then he parted her legs again, thrusting inside her, his movements measured to tease and entice.

She rose up from the mattress, the sheets clutched between her fingers as she met his thrusts, reaching for that last plateau. When it crashed through her, she screamed his name, then held him close, weeping against his chest.

He shuddered against her as he emitted a guttural groan. Then he rolled over, clasping her sweat-slick body close to his side. His chest rose and fell with deep, gasping breaths. "Oh, Ariel…"

The tears kept falling. She couldn't stop them; they ran unchecked down her face.

"Are you okay?" he asked, his voice deep with concern as he brushed away the tears. But more fell, trickling over his fingers.

She nodded.

"I didn't hurt you?"

She shook her head. "No. You were exactly what I needed." To release all the emotions churning inside her. To stop her thinking and worrying and just to make her feel.

As he stroked her cheek, his finger scraped over the slight ridge of her scratch. "I'm sorry the ring hurt you."

Ariel lifted her hand, blinking away the tears to stare at the diamond. "It's so big."

He entwined his fingers with hers. "Should I get it resized?"

She shook her head. "That's not what I meant. The band fits."

"But not the ring?" he surmised, his jaw taut. "You don't like it."

A sigh slipped from between her lips. "It's beautiful, David."

"But?"

She drew a quick breath back in and decided to be honest. "It's too much. Too valuable."

"Don't worry about that." He dipped his head, nuzzling her hair. "It's insured."

A smile teased her lips at his practicality. Of course he would have taken out insurance. To him, the ring was probably an investment. To her, it was a commitment she wasn't ready to make. "I really shouldn't be wearing it until I can give you an answer."

"You can take all the time you want, Ariel," he insisted.

Guilt nagged at her. "But I don't feel right about wearing it…."

"You're just not used to wearing rings." His fingers slid up her hand, then entangled with the silver chain around her wrist. "This is all the jewelry you ever wear. Who gave you this?" he asked as he caught the little pewter sun between his fingers.

"My mother." She swallowed hard. "She gave one to each of us the night the authorities took us away from her."

To protect them. Again she fervently prayed that Elena and Irina still had theirs.

"They gave her the time to do that?" he asked. "To say goodbye?"

Ariel shook her head. "She did it before they came." Through the field with their flashlights, as the men must have come with their torches all those years ago for her ancestor.

"It's almost like she knew," David mused.

It was exactly as if she'd known. But Ariel couldn't tell him about her mother's gift without telling him about her own. The admission burned in her throat, but she couldn't utter the words. She'd kept her secret for so long, using it to keep everyone at arm's length. Lovers. Friends. She'd never grown as close to anyone as she had David.

She couldn't lose him. Not now, not when she had

no one else. After they found her sisters, she'd tell him. Maybe she was exactly like her mother, using a man's wealth and power for protection. And like her mother, she'd undoubtedly wind up all alone.

Although David had promised he was looking for them, Ariel couldn't leave finding her sisters to anyone else, not even the man she loved. Despite the years that had passed since she'd seen them, the bond was there, pulling at her. She'd do anything to track them down and warn them, even attend a funeral.

Like David, Ariel had used the Internet, finding the obituary for Marie Cooper that had stated where and when services would be held for her. Standing discreetly in a corner of the small, rural funeral home in Armaya, she fingered the charm dangling from her wrist and remembered her mother saying that she didn't listen. Her mother, who hadn't believed in rules and hadn't given Ariel and her sisters any to follow, hadn't been referring to disobedience. She had to be referring to this...curse. What could Ariel hear if she'd learned to listen?

She would probably have been able to find her sisters by now without skulking around in the shadows of a funeral home, a black shawl covering the red hair that set her apart from the other mourners. The dozen or so people gathered were probably townspeople. None of them bore the Gypsy looks of her mother and aunt. The shawl wasn't enough for Ariel to blend in with them. In such a small town, everyone knew everyone else, so they all pegged her as a stranger. While they avoided her and lowered their voices, she still caught their whispers, questions about her identity. But they didn't just wonder about her; they made comments about her mother, too. Ariel could hear the living, sometimes even when they didn't want her to.

"I can't imagine why Myra isn't here. Marie was her sister."

"One of the few Coopers left," an elderly man remarked.

How many were left? Ariel needed to know. Were any of them among the mourners?

"Myra of all people should have *known*." The woman's voice held more acceptance than disdain. They knew of Myra's special ability. Since rejection hadn't driven her from Armaya, fear must have.

"That's who you are," the last woman said, turning toward Ariel. "I can't believe it…"

Caught, she wasn't about to run away, not when she had so many questions. She lowered the shawl so that her long red hair spilled over her shoulders. Heads swiveled, conversation ceased, as all attention focused on her.

She'd thought the mourners might respond better to a stranger than an outcast. If any of the Coopers had wanted her, they'd had nine years to pick her up from foster care. They hadn't come to her aid then, and she didn't harbor much hope that they would help her now. But for her sisters, she had to try.

"You're Myra's daughter," the woman spoke again. "The middle one."

"You don't even know my name." It had been more than two decades, and the family was distant. She shouldn't have expected anyone to remember her name, but disappointment pressed against her heart and stole her breath away.

"I'm not a Cooper, just a neighbor," the woman explained. "Myra only brought her daughters home a couple of times. She never stays in one place very long."

That wasn't the case anymore. But where was her body that these people didn't know that she'd died? They couldn't see her mother floating near the doorway, in the thick smoke highlighted by the amber glow of the orange light, with the woman who'd been hanged. No one else looked toward them as Ariel did. No one else seemed aware of anyone…but Ariel.

The woman reached out, startling Ariel as she slid her leathery fingers through her hair. "I remember you because of your hair. It was so beautiful. Still is."

The compliment didn't soften Ariel's resentment toward these people. Her hair often garnered compliments, from her sweet students, from David.

"Are there any Coopers here?" Ariel asked, speaking to all the mourners who had gathered around them, staring at her.

The woman who'd touched Ariel's hair glanced around the faces as if searching for someone. If she looked for Myra, she wouldn't find her—alive. She shook her head.

"Do you remember my sisters?" Ariel asked, her voice catching as her desperation grew.

"It's been a while," the woman qualified. "But, yes. Myra was a close friend. We would visit when she came to town. I remember her daughters. The skinny blond girl, she was the oldest. And the baby, she was the spitting image of your mama."

"I need to find them. Now." Before they wound up in a casket, like the woman behind her, whose body reclined against satin while her spirit hovered in mist.

"You don't know where your sisters are?"

Obviously not everyone in town knew they'd been taken away from Myra, then given up for adoption. Tears burned Ariel's eyes, but she refused to give in to the weakness. "No, I don't."

"I'm sure your mother can tell you."

Ariel shook her head. "My mother *can't* tell me anything anymore." Not so that she could understand.

The woman's forehead wrinkled. "I'm sure if Myra were here…"

Ariel didn't care what these people thought of her. "She's here," she said, gesturing toward her glowing ghost. "She's dead."

An awed murmur moved through the mourners. The woman stepped back from Ariel, her dark eyes wide with fear. "You have the curse."

Even though they weren't Coopers, they knew about it. She nodded. "And that's how I know I need to find my sisters." She raised her voice. "Does anyone know where they are?"

The woman shook her head, her eyes now soft with sympathy. "Your mother was the one who always knew things…before they happened. I grew up with her and her sisters."

"Sisters?" She remembered the pictures in the old farmhouse of three little gypsy girls. "Where's her other sister?"

"She lives here in Armaya."

The tears threatened again, from the sting of more rejection. Neither aunt had wanted her. Ariel drew in a shaky breath. "You knew them…tell me…"

"What?" the woman asked.

"Why wouldn't Marie or this other one—"

"Sadie."

"Why wouldn't they have taken me or my sisters?"

The woman shrugged. "I didn't know Myra had lost you. She was the only one of the three of them who could have children. That was why her mother gave her the charms."

The little pewter sun brushed Ariel's wrist as she twisted the shawl in her fingers. Somehow it all kept coming back to the charms. "What do you know…about them?"

The woman shivered even in the warm, stale air of the funeral home. "Your mother told terrible stories of witches and persecution. Some of it was from the past. Some from the future. That's why she ran. She was always so afraid."

Ariel remembered the fear. It lived in her own heart. She nodded. "I need to find this other aunt, Sadie."

"Someone else asked," the woman said.

"Who?"

She shook her head. "I don't know. He called here last night during the first visitation, and the receptionist called me to the phone since Sadie had already left. I figured he was a lawyer looking for next of kin."

Urgency sent Ariel's pulse racing. "Tell me where she lives."

The woman nodded. "I'll give you directions.

But first…your mother was my friend. I haven't seen her in a while, but I knew her well…."

Ariel bit her lip, waiting for whatever the woman felt she needed to say.

"If she gave you up," she said softly, "I'm sure she did it to keep you safe."

Ariel turned toward her mother's ghost hovering in the smoke near her sister's casket. *Mama, we're not safe anymore.*

Ariel pressed on the accelerator, forcing the Jeep to speed over the rutted country road. She knew it was dangerous going alone. The killer might still be there, might even be waiting for her, but she had no time to call David, and from the way the sheriff's deputy had treated her aunt's hanging, she doubted they would believe she needed help.

So when she stopped the Jeep in front of a small frame bungalow on the outskirts of town, she reached inside her purse for her canister of pepper spray. Then she stepped out and noticed the van already parked in the gravel driveway, its once glossy black paint coated with dust.

Was David here? Had his computer searches brought him to this house? Or had he been the man who'd called the funeral home? Instead of relief at the thought of his being inside, fear fluttered through her stomach. She swallowed it down; she couldn't suspect David had anything to do with the witch hunt. He didn't even know about it because she hadn't told him.

He was probably just questioning the woman about Ariel's sisters, as she planned to do. But then the sudden wail of approaching sirens renewed her sense of urgency. Heart hammering, she rushed inside. "David!"

The small kitchen was empty but for the dishes piled in the rusted sink. Her boot heels caught on the worn linoleum as she ran toward the back of the house, where something crashed onto the floor, rattling the windows as it shook the house.

Ariel drew up short in the doorway of the room where David leaned over a bed, pushing rocks onto the floor. "What are you doing here—" Then she glimpsed the hand sticking out of the pile, the fingers wiggling. Someone was underneath the mound of heavy stones struggling to survive. "Oh, my God!"

"Ariel," he said without looking up. His hands shook as he reached for another rock. "She's still alive. Help me!"

Ariel rushed across the room and joined David, her hands burning as she struggled to lift off the rocks. "Are we hurting her?" she asked, first-aid lessons running through her mind. You weren't supposed to move an accident victim.

But then, this was no accident. Someone had piled the rocks atop this poor woman, attempting to crush her to death, as they had witches centuries ago.

"She can't breathe," David said, grunting as he worked a particularly large rock off the pile. "We need to remove the pressure."

His knuckles oozed blood as he worked, not stopping even when the rescue crew arrived. He was stronger, bigger and younger than the aging volunteers. So probably was Ariel, but David sent her away.

"Get out of here," he ordered her as he reached for the rocks where the woman's head might lay.

"David—"

"Get out!"

Something about his commanding tone had her stumbling back. But she wasn't fast enough. Before she could turn away, she glimpsed the woman's disfigured face. "Oh, dear God…"

And she knew…she'd be seeing her again. Soon.

"Damn her!" he raged, wincing at the volume of his curse. Pain hammered at his temples and the base of his skull, relentless. Like the redhead.

She'd gotten close. Too damned close.

Just as that first witch had to his long-dead

ancestor. She'd gotten under his skin, into his heart. She'd known all his secrets. She could have destroyed him, the way the fire had destroyed his family. So he'd had to destroy her first.

Anger coursed through him, and he reached out with his hands, scraped raw from the rocks. Ignoring the blood oozing from his fingers and the pain radiating up his arms, he grabbed at something, anything, on his desk, flinging the journal across his office. The leather-bound book struck the wall with such force that its spine cracked and pages fluttered to the floor, the burned parchment shattering like glass.

"That bitch!"

The damned redheaded witch was destroying his plans and now his heritage. He hurried across the office and dropped to his knees on the hardwood floor. His swollen fingers fumbled the fragile papers. The burned edges had dissolved into ashes, the written words scrambled incoherently.

He dragged in a deep breath, trying to calm himself. It didn't matter if the journal was gone, the memories were his now. They were a part of him. He wouldn't lose them. He wouldn't be like the rest of his family and dismiss the McGregor legacy. He wouldn't lose his focus.

The witches would die.

He drew in another breath, reminding himself he was using the redhead to lead him to her sisters. All he had to do was wait.

But time was a luxury he didn't have. The doctors claimed it wouldn't be long now. If only he'd known about the power of the charms earlier, their protective and healing properties…

He shook his head, pain reverberating inside his skull at the simple gesture. It wasn't too late. Not for him. But soon, it would be too late for them.

Then he'd be the one laughing. He'd be the one with all the power.

Chapter 7

She'd never seen David so furious. His body radiated tension, nearly crackling like lightning, as his feet pounded the stairs on his descent from the upper level of the penthouse. They'd driven separately to the Towers, him beating her from the hospital by several minutes. He'd had time to find an outlet for his anger—a wall to punch, a wastebasket to kick.

She'd figured he must have since he hadn't had the guard stall her in the lobby this time. But his brow was as furrowed, his jaw as taut as it had been at her aunt's house and at the hospital. Ariel followed in the wake of his stomp toward the living room. He already had a crystal decanter in his hand and was pouring a drink from the bar in the corner when she caught up with him.

"They think she'll live, David," she reminded him of the young doctor's optimistic pronouncement, not certain she believed it even as she repeated it. "You found her in time. Now tell me *how* you found her and why you didn't tell me you had."

He took a deep swallow, then set the glass down with such force the crystal clinked against the glass-topped coffee table. "I pulled up a bunch of records on the Internet. Found birth certificates. Marriage licenses. This aunt of yours was married and divorced."

"Her last name wasn't Cooper?"

He shook his head as he picked up the glass again. "I didn't tell you because I couldn't reach you."

Out of respect, Ariel had shut off her cell phone at the funeral home.

"So you know how *I* found her. How did *you?*"

"I went to the other woman's funeral." She couldn't refer to them as her aunts; she didn't know them. But then, she didn't know her sisters either, not anymore. What were *they* to her? "I found out there was another Cooper left." Besides her. Her sisters weren't Coopers anymore. She only wished she knew what they were.

His fingers tightened around his glass until his

knuckles turned white. "You put yourself in danger, Ariel, just like you did for Haylee."

"That's why you're so mad." She'd known it and guilt nagged at her. She would do nothing but disrupt his life, bring to it the media attention he abhorred. Undoubtedly someone from the hospital had already phoned a reporter—the story was too sensational not to repeat. When it was discovered that David Koster had been the first on the scene, it would be more newsworthy and the press would be camped out around the Towers again. With a fingertip she twirled his ring on her finger, thinking of slipping it off and giving it back.

"Of course it's why I'm so mad!" he shouted, his deep voice vibrating.

Guilt flared again, over worrying him, not over what she'd done. "I am not going to apologize for trying to find my sisters."

He turned toward her, his eyes full of anger. "How stupid do you think I am, Ariel?"

For the first time his anger alarmed her, had her heart beating fast with nerves. "David…"

"You've had years to look for your sisters. Why now?" He uttered a short, derisive chuckle. "I thought it might have to do with my proposal. That you wanted to find them before you could give me an answer." He laughed again, the deep notes resonating with bitterness off the marble floor and high, plaster ceiling.

"David…"

He flung the glass, sending it hurling into the fireplace. "What the hell is going on, Ariel!"

Her heart thudded against her ribs. She knew the time had come to tell him *everything*. But she didn't know where to begin.

"First your older aunt, hanging…" His dark eyes flickered with emotion. "That was no accident, Ariel."

She drew in a quick breath. "How—how do you know?"

"There was no chair nearby that she could have kicked over. There wasn't one anywhere near her." He waved his hand around, gesturing toward the ceiling. "How do you hang yourself from a beam that high without climbing onto a chair first?"

Logical. He was always so logical. He would never understand what she had to tell him.

"Then your other aunt…" His chest rose and fell as he expelled a ragged breath. "Someone piled those rocks on top of her. Someone tried crushing her…alive."

"But you saved her," she said, although she didn't know how long the woman could survive after the trauma—the torture—she'd suffered. If not for David…

She needed him to help her save her sisters. He couldn't reject her now, not the way everyone else had. He'd said he loved her. But then so had many others....

He shook his head, then ran a shaking hand through his mussed blond hair. Blood from his scraped fingers streaked his forehead and stained his hair. "She's in a coma, Ariel. The doctors don't know for sure that she'll ever come out of it."

Her brain had been deprived of too much oxygen as her crushed ribs had punctured her lungs. Ariel rubbed her arms, thinking of the horror her aunt had endured. And she might never be able to tell them who had tried to kill her.

She swallowed hard, then began her story. "My two aunts, they weren't the first...."

His forehead furrowed, the blood highlighting the lines of bewilderment. "What?"

She told him what had happened three hundred and fifty years ago when the vendetta had spurred the beginning of the witch hunt.

He shrugged, his shoulders rippling beneath the black cashmere sweater he wore, the expensive garment stained with blood and dirt. "That's a legend, Ariel. You don't know if it's true or folklore passed down from generation to generation through your family."

So logical. There was no way he would understand.

"The killing has started again," she insisted. "In *this* generation, my mother was the first to die."

"I thought you hadn't seen her—"

"I haven't seen her—" she paused before adding "—alive."

"Ariel." His deep voice was amazingly calm and steady, his dark gaze watchful. "What are you trying to tell me?"

She drew a deep, steadying breath. "I hadn't seen her in more than twenty years, not since that night we were taken from her. Until the night you proposed."

"Ariel, you just said you haven't seen her. You're not making any sense…." And she was scaring him. She could see it in his eyes, an uneasy trace of fear churning in the dark depths.

"I'm not crazy," she defended herself. "That's what most people think, though, when they know the truth about me."

David dragged in a deep breath. "So what *is* the truth, Ariel?"

Something in his tone caught her attention, had her studying his handsome face. Her pulse kicked up speed, racing, as a realization came over her. "You already know."

Now she was scared…of what might happen to

her heart. "Of course you would know. It wouldn't take you long to hack into sealed records. Or maybe you broke into the social services office and looked in my file." After all, Margaret had told her that someone had looked at her record, before David had gone to Armaya with her. Had it been as Margaret suggested—a rich man checking out the woman he hoped to marry?

His brows rose in confusion as his chin lifted with pride. "I didn't break into any office. You asked me to find your sisters. I had to look up the files."

That had been *after* finding Marie.

"But you haven't found my sisters' adoption records." Or if he had, he hadn't told her.

"I can't get into them. Those files are better protected—"

"Than mine," she finished for him. She knew what her records contained, what had been said about her. Tears of frustration burned her eyes, and although she tried, she couldn't fight them. They slid down her face.

"So what is the truth, Ariel?" he asked again.

"That I love you." Would he believe it? Or would he think she was like her mother, only after his money?

Although it was the first time she'd professed it, he ignored her declaration of love, waving it off with a bloody hand. "Why didn't you *trust* me, Ariel? Why didn't you tell me about your past before?"

She shrugged, her shoulders aching with the slight movement. Like his, her hands were scraped raw, oozing blood through the swollen flesh. They'd worked so hard to free her aunt. She prayed the woman lived. She prayed David understood. "You read my file—you know why. Every time I told someone what I could do, what I saw, they got rid of me."

His dark eyes softened as his arms reached out for her. "Ariel…"

She jumped back, his pity hitting her like a slap. Her chin rose as anger whipped through her. "Don't do that," she warned him with quiet fury. "Don't feel sorry for me, the poor, crazy, abandoned girl."

"Ariel—"

"I don't want your pity. And I'm not crazy." She laughed now, with a hint of rising hysteria. "God, I wish I was. Then it wouldn't be real. I wouldn't really be able to see ghosts."

His Adam's apple bobbed as he swallowed hard. "Tell me about it."

She blew out a ragged breath. "I should have told you already. I intended to, but I was scared."

"That I would leave you?"

"That you wouldn't understand. It sounds so unbelievable. I don't expect you to—"

"That's how you knew Haylee was dead."

She nodded. "I saw her ghost. She came to school that day, like any other day. I still see her." Although the last time had been at the little girl's grave. "Maybe she knows I'm in danger. Maybe that's why she's stayed around. Otherwise they usually appear to me just after they've passed, when they're caught between this world and the next. Not that I help them get to it. I really don't do anything for them but *see* them. I can't *hear* them." She finally drew another breath as frustration burned a hole in her stomach like an ulcer.

A muscle ticked in David's tightly clenched jaw. "You're in danger?"

"I told you the legend," she reminded him. "Don't you get it? The hanging, the crushing. Someone's started a witch hunt."

"Ariel, that's—"

"What, David? Crazy?" she asked, her voice rising again with that thin note she hated. "I told you I've seen my mother." And she saw her again as the smoke filtered into the room, glowing with the orange light. "She's dead. Someone murdered her, too, like her sister."

"I didn't find a death certificate, so you're saying her body hasn't been found?"

Anger drew her lips tight. "Right. But it doesn't matter. I *know* she's dead." She drew in another breath before asking the most important question. "Do you believe me?"

He paced over to the fireplace, where shards of his broken liquor glass reflected the flames burning in the hearth. "God, Ariel, it's the twenty-first century. What you're talking about…"

"It's real, David. It's happening. My mother lived in fear of it. I think that's why she signed off her parental rights, to keep us safe." Or so she hoped. But she couldn't hear the woman, whose mouth moved, speaking words Ariel fervently wished she could hear.

"So you're saying someone from that family— what was their name?"

"McGregor." Despite how long ago she'd been told it, the legend was still clear in her mind. Indelible. Was it that she had a good memory or was it as her mother had claimed, that the charm helped her remember? Ariel held it between her fingertips, only now aware that she'd been stroking it during their entire conversation.

"You're saying a McGregor has resurrected this vendetta? That they want revenge on the Coopers?"

"Durikkens. We were Durikken women back then."

"Three hundred and fifty years ago?"

The way he said it, his voice all vague and confused, made it sound ridiculous. Pride stinging, she lifted her chin. "Yes."

"But Ariel, why now? If this vendetta's been ongoing, why aren't you all dead already?"

"I told you my mother gave us up—"

"But your aunts, they stayed in Armaya and until now they weren't harmed. Nobody was after them. And what about your grandmother? For that matter, what about that first Elena?"

"I don't know!" she shouted. "The charms—they protected the first Elena. She got away. As for the others, I'm not sure. Maybe no McGregor was crazy enough to kill…until now."

David shook his head.

"So you don't believe me?"

He sighed and dragged his hand through his hair again. "I don't know what to believe."

Her heart clenched, suspecting he wasn't referring just to the curse. "David…"

"I wish you would have told me all of this sooner."

"I couldn't risk it. I couldn't risk what we have." She hoped they still had it.

"Why couldn't you trust it?" he challenged her, his voice shaking. "That it was strong enough—"

"Is it?"

He walked across the living room toward her, not

stopping until he was close. Then he reached out, touching her face as he often did. With his thumbs, he brushed her tears away. "Don't you know how much I need you in my life? How much I love you?"

She stared into his eyes, searching his face for any sign of that pitying look. "But you think I'm crazy now."

He shook his head, then grimaced as if in pain. "No, Ariel, you're not the crazy one...."

"And you are?" she asked. "Why? For caring about me after you learned what I was keeping from you?" She couldn't imagine what he first must have thought when he'd read her file, what he might still think. "I'm not like my mother," she insisted. "I love you for you."

"Not my money."

"So you did wonder...."

He laughed, a weary, bitter chuckle. "Actually, no. I never did. You're not the kind of woman who cares about material things." He sighed. "God, it would be easier if you were...then I could be sure you'd never leave me."

She reached up and linked her arms behind his neck. "I *won't* leave you, David."

He sighed. "Maybe not by choice..."

So he believed her about the witch hunt, that someone wanted to kill her. She stiffened her spine, not having the time to give in to fear. "That's why we have to find my sisters, David, before something happens to them."

"We will," he promised.

She couldn't believe that he still wanted to help her, that he hadn't thrown her out instead. Dare she hope that for the first time in her life someone had accepted her as she was?

"Nothing will happen to your sisters," he reassured her. But he couldn't know that.

"Something might have already happened to them," she pointed out.

"If it had, you'd know, Ariel," he reminded her. "You would have *seen* them."

Her hope grew, lifting her heart, not only about her sisters but about her future with David. "You can really accept that I see people who've died?"

His eyes darkened to black. "We all live with ghosts."

Ariel awoke alone again in David's bed with her clothes on. He'd acted as though he'd accepted what she'd told him about herself, but he hadn't touched her last night. His dark eyes soft with sympathy, he'd told her to go up to bed.

Naively she'd believed he would join her later, after he shut off the lights downstairs. But she'd turned her head on the pillow and found no indent in the one next to hers, the satin sheets iron-smooth on the other side of the bed, not tangled, like the ones around her restless legs. She couldn't remember dreaming, but maybe she'd been running in her sleep, trying to escape a killer.

With a trembling hand, she pushed her hair, sticky with perspiration, off her forehead, then blinked to bring the clock into focus and read the illuminated numbers. Two in the morning. Where was David? She kicked off the sheets and stumbled toward the door. If he couldn't deal with what he'd learned about her, she would rather leave than sleep in his bed without him.

Shadows loomed in the hall as the mini chandeliers burned low, casting little light. She checked the guest rooms, fumbling for light switches to see if he had slept in one of the beds, but they were empty.

That left only his office on this floor. Her hand trembled as she reached for the knob, but before she attempted to turn it, a murmur of voices drifted from under the door like smoke. Two men argued, one voice raspy, the other deep. Ty and David.

Had David called Ty over in the middle of the night? And Ty had come. Once again the nature of their friendship humbled her. Because she'd never really been able to trust someone not to think she was crazy or reject her, she'd never had a friend as close as these two were. But if they were so close, why did anger vibrate with their words?

"What the hell's going on?" Ty asked.

"You don't need to know all the details yet," David insisted as if he were doing Ty a favor.

But the favor he was doing was probably for Ariel, keeping the secrets she'd kept from him for so long. Her heart thumped hard, moved by her love for David. Then shame washed over her that she was invading the privacy he held so dear. She shifted on her feet, lifting her hand at the same time, undecided between stepping away or making her presence known by knocking.

"You actually *believe* Ariel?" Ty asked, drawing her attention again with the mention of her name. "You think she can really see dead people?"

So he hadn't kept her secret. Well, she should have expected he'd share it with his best friend. She held her breath, waiting for David's response, knowing that he would offer the truth more freely to Ty than he might to her.

But he didn't answer either question, just expelled a ragged sigh before saying, "Right now my main concern is that she doesn't wind up dead like her aunt."

"Of course," Ty agreed. "I'll do whatever you want."

"Good. I'll owe you."

"C'mon, you know we'll never be even. I can never repay you for…"

For what? Ariel leaned her head against the wood, the door creaking in the frame. She drew in an unsteady breath, worried that they might discover her eavesdropping but too interested to walk away. They talked about her, so she had a right to know if they both thought she was crazy or delusional.

"I want something else from you," David told his friend, his voice a solemn rumble that raised goose bumps on Ariel's skin.

"Anything," Ty said. "You know it."

"I want a gun."

A short chuckle emanated from Ty. "No, you don't. I know how you feel about them." The rasp of his voice grew more hoarse with shock. "You can't be serious."

"This situation is serious, Ty."

So he did believe her about the witch hunt. She felt no satisfaction in that, though, not since he felt the need to arm himself. She'd done this to him, brought chaos and danger to his life. He didn't deserve this. Tears burned her eyes, blinding her.

"But, David—"

"I need a gun. I need you to get me one right away—"

"What the hell's going on?" Ty repeated.

Ariel didn't wait to see if David answered him this time. She stepped back from the door, then hurried down the hall toward the stairs. She held her breath as each mahogany step creaked during her descent. The doors to the elevator stood open. She slipped through the foyer, grabbed her purse from a table and stepped into the mirrored car.

"I'm sorry, David," she whispered. Not for leaving now but because she hadn't left sooner.

Elena Jones-Phillips jerked upright in bed, panting heavily. She reached for her husband, needing the comfort of his arms, but his side of the bed was empty, as it often was. She remembered his business trip, another out-of-town one, compliments of his boss. But Elena couldn't think about that tyrant or about her husband.

She couldn't think about anything but her dream. That was all it was. A bad dream. Nothing else. She flipped on the bedside lamp, the soft glow of the Tiffany lamp illuminating only a small circle of the blackness of Elena's bedroom, which mirrored the blackness of her mood.

She pressed her palms against her eyes, trying to

assuage the pain throbbing there, trying to blind her mind to what she'd seen. It was just a dream. None of it was real. Just a figment of an overactive imagination, brought on by stress. Or too much caffeine.

But even though she was awake, she saw it again. Like some of the other dreams, it was a murder. Although no thunder rumbled, lightning flashed through Elena's mind, cutting jaggedly across the screen inside her head where the murder played.

A woman was running, her long red hair streaming behind her, her mouth open in a scream before a big hand closed over it. No matter how many times the scene replayed in Elena's mind, the woman never got away. She never escaped him. He wrapped the rope around her neck, chafing the pale skin as he pulled the noose tight, then strung the rope over the beam. Only his arms were visible, his face hidden in shadows. Unidentifiable. He lifted her until her feet dangled, until the rope cut off her last breath, her turquoise eyes locked in a vacant stare.

"No…" Elena cried, choking against the pain as if the rope were cutting off *her* breath, ending *her* life. "Please, no…"

She didn't always dream of murder, just lately. Sometimes she dreamed of innocuous things, somehow anticipating something her husband might do. But he was a simple, predictable man.

The dreams were not predictable. She had no inclination of when one was coming on or what or whom she might dream about.

She wanted to believe this redheaded woman a stranger, someone unknown and unconnected to Elena. But even though it had been twenty years, Elena recognized the child she'd known in the woman she now saw.

Ariel. Breathtakingly beautiful. Even in death…

Chapter 8

Ariel held her breath as she ducked under the yellow crime-scene tape and stepped into the bedroom, averting her eyes from the rocks strewn about the floor. The boards shifted beneath her feet, sending a rock tumbling across the scarred oak.

Nerves fluttered in her stomach as fear gripped her. She didn't know how many rules she was breaking, but she didn't care. This woman's house might hold a clue to her sisters' whereabouts, and Ariel's determination to find them blinded her to the law.

But she wasn't blind to the mist, which hung heavily in the room. The light shone faintly, leaving the ghost of the disfigured woman in shadows. As Ariel had suspected, the young doctor had been overly optimistic. Sadie Cooper hadn't survived the night.

Skirting the area around the bed, Ariel headed toward a desk tucked into a corner of the small room. Like the one at Marie's house, the drawers had been pulled open, the contents riffled through. Postcards from Myra lay face up on the blotter and the floor below the desk, the symbols of star, moon and sun circled on all of them.

What had Myra really meant when she'd encircled those symbols below her signature? Unite them? The charms or the children? She'd had twenty years and never attempted to get them together, until now, until they were in danger.

As at Marie's house, the only things of interest to Ariel were those postcards. The other papers were junk mail or old bills. David had found more information online searching birth certificates and marriage licenses. But there'd been no marriages for Myra, and all the fathers of her daughters were listed as unknown. Dead ends were literally all Ariel could find, but then, that was her curse.

She turned toward the bed, the sheets stained with blood and soil from the rocks. As she'd always done when she needed comfort, she reached for the sun charm dangling from her bracelet. The pewter warmed her fingertips and settled the nerves churning in her stomach. Was the charm's power only sentimental or something more?

While she contemplated that, she moved toward the bed. Another rock shifted as the bedroom floor groaned. The weight of the rocks must have weakened the old joists. Ariel stepped back just as the floor gave, splitting apart as one of the rafters splintered and broke. The rocks rumbled as they rolled toward the center, widening the crack, so that some spilled through, crashing to the basement floor below. Dust rose like smoke, teasing Ariel's nose into a sneeze. The shift of weight broke the floorboard beneath one of her feet. Fear of falling to the basement froze her in place, her lungs burning as she held her breath and the little pewter charm.

But the dust settled, the floor no longer creaked. Only the one rafter had broken, causing the rift. She expelled a ragged sigh, wondering if dumb luck or the charm had saved her from a painful fall.

The charms will keep you safe. Her mother's words rang in her head.

After pulling her foot from the broken floorboard, Ariel walked slowly and carefully over to the little table serving as a nightstand. Inside she found an address book, but the only Cooper with a number listed was Marie.

She was gone. They were all gone now, that generation of Coopers. Hand shaking, Ariel lifted a trifold picture frame, like the one she'd seen at Marie's house, from the nightstand. Each section held a photo of a little dark-haired girl. The mist thickened around Ariel as if enclosing her in a protective shield. From somewhere outside the bedroom a floorboard creaked. The weight of the rocks would have no effect on other rooms. Ariel wasn't alone with the ghosts. Someone living and breathing moved around in the house.

Still clutching the picture frame, she scrambled around the cracked floor and ducked behind the bedroom door. Her heart hammered against her ribs as she fumbled her can of pepper spray from the front pocket of her jeans. Despite her close scrape with the floor, she still didn't have enough confidence in the charm to rely solely on it. Maybe once she found her sisters and the other charms. Somehow she knew she needed them to fight the killer, that she couldn't do it alone.

Could that be who else was in the house? The killer? But why return to the scene of his crime unless…he'd been following Ariel?

Her heart lurched as the stealthy footsteps neared the bedroom. She bit her lip, holding in the shuddery breath burning her lungs.

Then a voice rasped, "Ariel…"

He had followed her! Her fingers tightened around the can of pepper spray. She was counting on a blast of it giving her enough time to escape. Ariel would not meekly accept what her ancestor had called her fate.

The man called her name again. "Ariel?"

"Ty!" Relief flowed through her, weakening her knees so that she sagged to the floor.

A big hand closed around the edge of the door, pulling it away from her. "What are you—" His blue eyes narrowed as his gaze traveled from her face to the items she clutched. "So what were you going to hit me with—the can or the picture frame?"

Her heart thudding as the fear ebbed out of her, she managed to lift her lips in a smile. "Whatever it took…"

"Smart woman," he remarked, extending his hand to help her off the floor.

After tucking the pepper spray back into her pocket, she put her hand in his. "Not that smart since I didn't know you were following me."

He tugged her to her feet but wouldn't meet her gaze. "David asked me to."

So that had been the first favor David had asked of Ty, before he'd requested the gun.

"That was smart of him. He's not as good at following me."

Ty's gaze traveled from her to the crack in the floor and the rocks in it and those strewn around the room. "He's worried about you."

Her safety or her sanity?

"I can take care of myself," she maintained. She'd been doing it for twenty years.

"Come on, Ariel, a can of pepper spray isn't protection against a lunatic! Look at this place!" He gestured at the rocks and the bed stained with blood. "Whoever this nut is, he's already killed two women—"

"Three." She held the picture frame out for him to see the faces of the little girls. "Three sisters."

"You're sure your mother is dead?" he asked, as he glanced from the photos to her.

For some reason she didn't want to admit to eavesdropping on his conversation with David. When David had called her the next morning, she hadn't let on to him either, only saying that she'd left his house in the middle of the night because she needed to be alone for a while.

"I'm sure when David asked you to follow me, he told you everything." Why did she suspect he would not do the same with her? What secret was he keeping? Or was it just her lack of trust that had her suspecting he had one?

Then she remembered Ty's words that night. He

owed David. But that could have been for anything—he had come to live with David's family
after his father had died. She shook her head,
pushing away the doubts.

"So what do you think, Ty?" she prodded him to
break the uneasy silence that had fallen over them.

"Ariel…" Again Ty looked away from her,
focusing on the pictures instead.

"You think I'm crazy. I'm sure David does. He
won't admit it because he cares—"

"He loves you," Ty said, almost as if he were
disappointed. He probably thought David had lost
his mind, too.

"But does he *believe* me?"

Ty nodded. "He has me following you. He
believes you could be in danger."

Could be. She bit her lip as frustration tangled the
nerves in her stomach. Was that the only reason
he'd wanted the gun—because she could be? If he
didn't believe her about the witch hunt, he probably
didn't believe anything else either.

"I can see ghosts," she insisted. "I'm not crazy."

"Ariel, I didn't say—"

"You didn't have to." She sighed, expelling a
ragged breath.

He didn't argue with her, just said, "David called
me a few minutes ago. Your aunt died this morning."

"I know."

"They called you, too?"

She shook her head, her lips lifting in a rueful smile. "They didn't have to, Ty. I know when people have died."

Again he ignored her proclamation. "So is that why you're here?"

She nodded. "I'm hoping to find something to lead me to my sisters." Her fingers tightened on the polished brass frame of her mother and aunts. "We're the only Coopers left now. Three sisters, like these three."

"David said you haven't seen them in twenty years."

Tears burned her eyes, but she blinked them away. "I need to find them, Ty."

Strong fingers closed over her shoulder, offering a reassuring squeeze. "We will."

"How can you be so sure?"

"David's working on it. He *always* gets what he wants."

She shivered, the comment sounding less like a compliment and more like a warning. "Ty…"

He didn't lift his gaze to hers. Instead he stared at her hand where the diamond glinted in the afternoon sunshine. "He didn't tell me about your engagement."

She glanced down at the ring, guilt tugging at

her that she had yet to give David an answer. "It's not official."

He reached out, pressing his finger against the diamond. "You're wearing his ring."

"Yes, but I haven't said yes."

"Yet." His gaze finally met hers, his blue eyes deepening to navy. "You will."

She shook her head. "It's not my decision anymore."

"What do you mean?"

"David knows the truth about me now." She blinked hard, fighting against the threat of tears. "He might change his mind."

A corner of Ty's mouth tipped up into a crooked grin. "If only…"

She'd often thought Ty didn't consider her good enough for his best friend. Did his comment mean that or something more personal?

Then he chuckled. "Not a chance, not with what he's willing to do for you."

She wouldn't admit to knowing about the gun. "He's helping me find my sisters."

Ty nodded. "So tell me about them."

"My sisters? I don't know anything about them now. We were so young."

"Do they have any—" his throat moved as he swallowed, then whispered "—gifts?"

"I don't know. When we were little, they never really said." As a child, when she'd seen the ghost of her grandma, she'd never mentioned it to her sisters. Or her mother. She hadn't been sure what was real and what wasn't, not with the con games her mother had played.

Her fingers stroked over the face of the little girl in the middle frame. Mama had been the middle sister, like Ariel. "My mother was the only one of her sisters to have gifts. What if I'm the only one? My sisters will have no warning that someone's after them until I find them."

Or the killer does.

Ty arched his scarred brow.

"You don't believe me," she accused him, fighting the frustration gripping her. Television personalities, both real and fiction, purported to have her gift. So why could no one accept that *she* had it? Was she not special enough to have an unusual ability?

Ty shook his head. "It's not that, Ariel."

"Then what?"

He shrugged. "From a police standpoint, I'd be more interested in finding the threat than your sisters. It's easier to find one person than two."

"You're saying I shouldn't be looking for Elena and Irina?"

He shook his head. "It might not be necessary—"

"Because you don't believe any of us are in danger?"

"I'd be a fool not to believe that." And Ty was no fool. "I'm saying you're looking for the wrong people. A cop doesn't go looking for more victims. He looks for suspects in the crimes that have already occurred."

She shuddered, hating to think of herself or her sisters as victims.

Ty continued his explanation. "You need to find the killer."

Ariel's pulse quickened at the jangle as keys turned in the lock of the front door. She wasn't worried that the killer had found her. She was worried about David.

Heavy footsteps trod through the archway, into the living room where Ariel sat in her favorite extra-wide easy chair, her laptop open across her knees. Warm breath blew across the nape of her neck, exposed by the high ponytail she wore. She closed her eyes as he brushed a soft kiss against her jaw. A shiver rippled through her at the delicious sensation of his lips against her skin.

He made it impossible for her to stay away from him, as she'd intended. She wanted to uncomplicate his life. "David…"

"You're mad at me," he said.

She tried to summon anger or, at the very least, righteous indignation. "I *should* be mad at you."

He sighed. "With everything going on, I wanted to make sure you were safe. But I know how independent you are."

Because she'd had to be. She'd never had anyone she could count on. She glanced down at her hand, at the glittering diamond. Dare she believe she had someone now? She closed her eyes, shutting out the ring and David. She couldn't involve him any deeper.

"I asked Ty to follow you because I didn't want to take any chances," he explained.

She used old hurts and bitterness to harden her voice. "In case someone *really* was after me?"

He shook his head, his soft hair brushing her cheek. "I'm not going to fight with you. You're not going to push me away again."

"I'd be doing you a favor," she told him.

His hands closed over her shoulders as he pressed his cheek against hers. "You're not getting rid of me that easily."

She might not, but what about the killer? Would he get rid of David if he continued to get in his way? It was a risk she didn't want to take. Not with David.

"What kind of future can we have when you don't believe me?" she reasoned.

"It's not that I don't believe you, but you don't

know for sure what really happened. Someone could have killed your aunts for another motive. For land. For money. Who knows?"

"That's why I have to find him."

"Him?"

"Her. I suppose the McGregor descendant could be female." She hadn't considered that possibility because of the strength it would have taken someone to lift the first aunt up to that beam and put all those rocks onto the second.

"That's what you're doing," he said, scanning her computer screen. "Looking up McGregors?"

"Trying to." She'd found so many she didn't know how to begin to narrow down her search.

"Why didn't you ask me to help you?"

She didn't want David getting hurt by anyone, least of all herself if she kept pushing him away, so she withheld the truth. Again. "You're already working on finding my sisters."

His breath sighed out in a ragged groan of frustration with which she could so identify. "I can't find any way to unseal their adoption records. I'm sorry."

"Me, too." She wanted to see her sisters again and not just to warn them. After how David had responded to her past, she was brave enough to risk their rejection now. She was stronger than she'd been at eighteen, when she'd first considered finding them.

"I'm not giving up, Ariel."

On finding her sisters or on them? She should give him an answer to his proposal. The one burning in her throat was yes, but she couldn't utter it, not just out of fairness to him but out of fear for herself. Maybe he'd changed his mind. Maybe she wasn't as brave as she thought.

He slid his arm around her as he moved to sit beside her on the oversize chair, but a file protruded from between the cushion and the side. "What's this?"

"You've seen it," she reminded him. "It's my record."

He fingered the worn manila folder. "You've had this for a while."

"A long time."

"You looked for your sisters before."

She nodded.

"Why did you give up?"

She took the folder from his hands and flipped through it, thumbing the pages like a fan. "There's nothing here to use to find them." The contents showed only how lost she'd been growing up. How alone.

"I'll admit I'm not sure about this whole witch hunt thing," David said. "All those McGregors could have died out long ago."

As the Coopers would if someone didn't stop killing them. "Then who murdered those women?"

David shrugged. "Another enemy, maybe someone using the vendetta to disguise their real motive."

Ariel sighed. "David, I haven't seen my mother in a long time and I don't remember my aunts. I don't know who their enemies might be."

"We'll look for them."

Ariel handed the laptop over to him. "You look." She stood up, stretching the kinks from her back and clutching her file. She hadn't looked at it in so long. But she was stronger now, she reminded herself. She thumbed through all the documents until she found the one she sought— the formal complaint that her mother was an unfit parent. Only an enemy would swear out such a complaint.

"Thora Jones."

"What?" David asked, glancing up from the computer.

"She was an enemy of my mother's."

"Who is she?"

Ariel shrugged. "Maybe a wife of one of the men my mother seduced. Or someone my mother swindled during a séance."

His forehead furrowed. "How's that?"

"Not only can I see ghosts, I used to play one for

my mother occasionally. Although she had real gifts, she used to con people." She laughed bitterly. "Claimed she was doing them a favor, that it was nicer to lie to them than tell them the truth. An old Gypsy proverb."

"Do you remember Thora Jones?"

"No." She shook her head. "But I was nine. I don't remember all that much."

"You remembered the legend."

She sighed. "It was the kind of thing that would make an impression on a child, give her night-mares for years afterward." Where she lay awake, crying and trembling with fear and no one to comfort her.

"Ariel…"

She jerked her chin. "No. No pity. Not from you."

His lips slowly pulled up into a grin.

"Thora Jones…" he said, changing the subject. As he repeated the name, his brow furrowed.

She nodded, hope flaring. "Do you know her?"

"Does it give her address?"

Ariel turned her attention back to the complaint, a sense of foreboding racing across her skin as she read the address. "Right here in Barrett."

"I thought I recognized the name."

"What if she's a McGregor, David?"

"Ariel, she swore out that complaint twenty years

ago. Like you said, she could have had any number of reasons for reporting your mother as unfit."

He didn't say it, but she called him on it. "Because she *was* unfit?"

His dark eyes softened with sympathy. "What you said about the séances and the men—it doesn't sound like the ideal environment for a child."

"It wasn't," she admitted, regret heavy on her heart. "But it was a lot better than what followed."

Even if Thora Jones wasn't a McGregor, Ariel wanted to give her a piece of her mind for stealing the only family Ariel had known. She reached down for her purse, which sat beside the couch, and rummaged inside for her keys. "I hope she still lives at the same address—"

"You're not going alone to see her," he said, his fingers closing over hers. "You're not pushing me away or shutting me out again, Ariel."

His fingers warmed her hand, his words her heart. She gazed up into his eyes at the twin reflections of herself in the dark orbs. He leaned over, brushing his mouth against hers once, twice, with just enough passion that she lost her breath.

"David, she's probably an old lady now. I'll be okay," she insisted.

He shook his head, unswayed by her argument. "I'm coming with you."

* * *

When they buzzed the intercom at the tall wrought-iron gates, gratefulness that she wasn't alone calmed some of the nerves jittering in Ariel's stomach. She might be braver now but not this brave.

Peering through the windshield of David's Escalade, she concluded that the sprawling four-story brick house didn't look like a private residence at all. Instead the imposing structure, the grounds entirely fenced, reminded her of the sanitariums where she'd been locked away from time to time growing up.

"Are you sure this is the right place?" she asked.

He nodded. "Yeah, the Jones estate. And you think my penthouse is cold."

She'd never told him that. How did he know her so well? "This really is a house?"

He laughed. "Everyone in Barrett but you knows the Jones estate. You don't care how much money people have."

And maybe he thought her crazier about that than about seeing ghosts.

"Have you changed your mind?" he asked, glancing over at her.

She shook her head, determined to face the person who had begun her nightmare.

"Do you have an appointment?" a voice squawked through the intercom.

"David Koster," he said, neither confirming nor denying if he had one.

With his position in Barrett, he didn't need reservations or appointments. Predictably the wrought-iron gates opened. Ariel realized again that it was a good thing David had come with her. Without him, she doubted she would have gotten inside.

Once he drove up to the imposing front door of aged oak and antique brass, she reached for his arm, closing her fingers around the green silk of his sleeve. "David, I want you to stay here. I *need* to do this by myself."

He turned toward her, his brown eyes dark with hurt. "Are you ever going to let me in, Ariel?"

She knew what he really meant—would she ever trust him? That was an answer she couldn't give either of them. But she could give him a bit more honesty. "David, you're further into my life than anyone's ever been."

His mouth kicked up into his little wicked grin, and his hand cupped her cheek, his fingers stroking over her skin. "I like to go further than anyone else."

"David…"

He put his hands back on the wheel, gripping it. "I'll stay here. But you stay outside where I can see you and make sure you're safe."

She might be safe physically, but she didn't think

she'd be very emotionally safe facing down the woman who'd destroyed her family, such as it'd been. Palm damp, she fumbled with the door handle before stepping out of the vehicle. Her boots tapped an uneven rhythm against the cobblestone driveway as she walked hesitantly to the front door. She found no doorbell, just a knocker in the shape of ram's head, but there must have been a hidden camera somewhere, because she'd barely lifted the heavy brass knocker when the door opened.

A blond woman stood before Ariel, her eerie light blue eyes dazed before she blinked and focused. "You're not David Koster."

"You're not Thora Jones." She was too young to have been the woman who'd accused Myra of being an unfit mother twenty years ago. She probably wouldn't have even been a teenager yet. Hair rose on the nape of Ariel's neck and her skin prickled. Could it be? Blond. With those unforgettable, eerie blue eyes. She looked like an aged-progression photograph of the image of the child in Ariel's mind.

Was this the woman her older sister had grown into? Except for the physical similarities, she had none of Elena's fire and charm Ariel remembered. This woman was a stranger. She matched the house, cold and unapproachable, in a gray blouse and flannel trousers. Ariel couldn't mistake her for a housekeeper, not with the diamonds at her ears and neck and the imperious tilt of her nose and chin.

"Thora is my grandmother. She's not available right now." She stepped back as if to close the door again, dismissing Ariel.

"You're Elena Cooper." The words spilled from Ariel's lips like an accusation.

The chin tilted again, and despite being shorter than Ariel, she managed to look down her thin nose at her. "I'm Elena Jones-Phillips."

Her surname was inconsequential. What mattered was that Ariel had found her older sister.

Chapter 9

Ariel's heart clenched as she realized that, while she had grown up with strangers, Elena had been living with family, the woman responsible for their mother's losing custody of them. Instead of fighting Thora Jones's charge, Myra had just given up. She'd given up *them*.

Ariel's knees weakened. She couldn't believe that after all these years and all her fears she'd found her sister like this, almost by accident.

"Who are you?" Elena asked with a faint quaver in her voice, as if afraid of the answer.

"You know who I am," Ariel said, realizing the

dazed look in Elena's pale blue eyes when she'd opened the door had been recognition. And shock. As Ariel had anticipated when she was eighteen, her sisters—at least this one—wanted nothing to do with her. Pain squeezed her heart, and she fought a silent battle for her breath…and her pride. Finding both, she straightened and remarked, "Good thing I'm not here for a tearful reunion."

"Then why are you here?"

"To warn you."

Thick black lashes blinked over those blue eyes once, then again. "About?"

"The curse."

Blond hair brushed the woman's shoulders as she shook her head. "You're talking about the ramblings of an unstable woman. None of that was true," she insisted, her voice vibrating with intensity. "It was all in her alcohol- and drug-induced imagination. Curses, vendettas, special abilities—none of that was *real*."

"I've thought that sometimes." When she'd awakened from a nightmare, soaked with sweat. "Then I would look at this." Ariel lifted her wrist, dangling the sun charm near Elena's face.

Elena lifted her wrists, both bare but for the slim gold watch on her right one. "It's been twenty years. I've forgotten everything about that life." Her mouth twisted into a hard line as she added, "And everyone."

Ariel resisted the urge to lash out. Nothing of the girl she'd known and loved was left in this cold, hard woman. But because she had loved the girl, she had to warn her. "Well, someone hasn't forgotten about us. Or the curse. We're the only Coopers left. The others have been murdered."

Elena's breath caught audibly as her face paled. "Irina?"

"I don't know."

"Mother?"

Ariel nodded and fought the tears burning her eyes. She wouldn't shed them, not in front of this stranger. But could a ghost cry? Her mother hovered near them, enveloped in smoke and orange light, and Ariel thought she glimpsed something glistening on the woman's near-transparent face. She'd grown used to her mother's appearance, but she studied Elena for any reaction to the apparition.

Elena's slender throat noticeably moved as she swallowed. But no fear widened her eyes. She obviously couldn't see their mother. "Was there a funeral?"

"Not yet." Ariel sighed, then admitted, "No one's found her body yet."

Her sister looked at her, surprise on her face. "But you know…"

Ariel bobbed her head. "I see them…all of them…who've died."

Elena shook her head. "No, that's not possible. You're like Mother. You're making it up or imagining it. I can't go through that again, wondering what's real and what's pretend. I can't have that in my life."

Even though Ariel had endured many rejections, she winced from the hurt, the pain pressing down on her chest as if her sister had stomped on it. She closed her eyes, holding back the tears she was too proud to shed. "Like I said, I didn't expect a tearful reunion."

"You just came to warn me." Her sister sniffed derisively. "It's been a while. I forgot how our mother played fools. Did she promise to ward off the evil spirits for a price? Is that what you want from me? Money?"

Ariel's palm itched with the temptation to slap her older sister's beautiful face. "I don't want your money."

Elena craned her neck, glancing around her until Ariel turned toward the black Escalade, too. David hadn't kept his promise—or at least he hadn't stayed behind the wheel. He stood outside the SUV, leaning against the driver's door, his arms crossed across his muscular chest. Dark glasses hid his eyes, and the light spring breeze played in his blond hair. "David Koster. I guess you don't need *my* money. Our mother taught you well. You're just like her."

Ariel shrugged off the insult. "I wouldn't know. I hadn't seen her in twenty years, not until I saw her ghost."

Elena bit her bottom lip, either over Ariel's claim or to hold back questions she wanted to ask. Despite her struggle, one slipped out. "You didn't go back to her…after that night?"

Ariel shook her head. "Nope. Neither did Irina. She got adopted, and I got bounced around foster homes until I was eighteen." Now she turned her attention to the house behind Elena, clicking her tongue as if impressed. "Looks like you had a softer landing than I did."

Elena's chin tipped up again. "If you don't want my money, what do you want?"

"Your help. I need to find Irina."

"To warn her, too? To disrupt her life? To scare her?" Elena fired the questions even though those pale eyes remained icy and indifferent.

"To save her life. If it's not too late. Do you have any idea who might have adopted her? Maybe she's with her paternal family, too. Did you know who her father is?"

"No."

"That's right. You've forgotten all about us." Ariel wrestled her frustration and pain to the side. She couldn't deal with it.

"You'd be smart to do the same," Elena advised. "Move on with your life. Forget about the past."

"*I* can't," she insisted. "A killer won't let me."

Elena's face remained closed, disbelieving. "I can't help you then," she said, stepping back into the foyer. Before she could swing the door closed, Ariel braced her palm against the heavy oak.

"Yes, you can."

"I don't have any special powers. Mother made up that story. It wasn't real, Ariel, no matter how much you want to believe that it was. Nothing about that life was real."

Ariel nearly believed her because the bond she'd thought forged between her and her sisters didn't exist anymore, if it ever really had.

"Okay. But I do need something from you...." The image of all those postcards, with the star, moon and sun in a circle flashed through Ariel's mind. She had no real proof, but somehow she knew those charms—like the sisters—needed to be reunited to finally vanquish the curse and the killer.

Elena sighed, then asked, "How much do you want?"

"For the last time, I don't want your money. I want your charm. The star."

The blond hair moved again as the woman shook her head. "I'm sorry."

"You won't give it to me?"

"That was a lifetime ago," she said, as if Ariel could have ever forgotten. "I don't have that trinket anymore."

Trinket. To her it had been a worthless piece of junk. To Ariel it had always been a cherished family heirloom. "It's gone?"

"Lost a long time ago," Elena admitted before closing the door in Ariel's face.

Without all the charms, Ariel suspected she would be the same. Lost. Fate, the vendetta and the killer would win.

David settled Ariel onto one of the leather couches, then started a fire in the marble hearth. But none of its warmth penetrated the chill that had her trembling. "You're shivering," he said, sliding his arm around her as he sat beside her.

"I think she gave me frostbite," she said, trying to ease the knot in her chest with humor, however forced.

His hand slid up from her shoulder to cup her face. "It was that bad?"

She nodded. "My sister is heartless, David."

His dark eyes widened but not with surprise. Ariel had told him on the drive to the Towers that she'd found Elena. "I don't know her, but I do remember hearing that Thora has a granddaughter named Elle. Thora Jones isn't a very warm woman. Her reputation is that she's cold and ruthless."

"Then her granddaughter is just like her."

He shrugged. "I'm sure the same has been said about me. You can't believe everything you hear or read."

"*She* doesn't believe anything," Ariel said, bitterness sour on her tongue. "She doesn't think the legend's real or that any of us have special abilities."

David didn't say anything; he probably agreed with Elena. Ariel's stomach churned. At least he hadn't rejected her, the way her older sister had. "She wants nothing to do with me, David."

His thumbs stroked her cheeks, brushing away the tears she hadn't realized had slipped from her eyes. "Maybe she's just afraid."

"Of what? She doesn't believe she's in danger." And that made her far more vulnerable, because she wouldn't be alert. She wouldn't be able to protect herself, not without the charm.

"She probably thinks you hate her."

Ariel's lips twisted into a grimace. "I don't. But she certainly didn't go out of her way to endear herself to me."

"She might have figured there was no use, that you blame her for what her grandmother did to your mother."

Ariel fisted her hands, wishing she'd met the infamous Thora Jones. But then, how could she blame the woman for wanting to save her granddaughter from the vagabond lifestyle of a con artist that no child should have lived?

"Elena was only twelve when we were taken away," Ariel said. "If she ever met her paternal grandmother before, it had to have been before I was born. She can't be held responsible for that woman's actions. Elena was just a kid."

"You all were."

That had been the last time she had felt like a child—in that little truck camper when their mother bestowed upon each of them a charm. Ariel fingered her little pewter sun. She couldn't imagine *not* wearing it.

"No, David, you're wrong. Elena's not worried about my blaming her for anything. She just doesn't want me in her life," Ariel said. "Because she doesn't want to remember where she came from. I can't believe that she…"

"What?" David prodded when she couldn't go on.

"She lost her charm." Or had thrown it away.

Had Irina? She'd been so young when Mama had given them the charms. She'd probably lost hers long ago. Just as Irina was lost to them. Maybe for eternity.

"You say that like it's a death sentence," David remarked, his eyes narrowed.

Ariel's breath burned in her lungs just as the orange light burned in the smoke, which surrounded her mother's ghost. The woman's dark eyes widened with fear, her mouth open as if she sobbed. Ariel had grown used to her; she hadn't even noticed when her mother reappeared.

"I think it might be. Mama said she gave the charms to us to keep us safe. At Marie's and Sadie's I found postcards from my mother. She signed her name, then drew the symbols of each charm and circled them. They're important, David, and I'm probably the only one left to still have hers."

Did that mean she would be the only to survive? Without the protection of the charm, would she have died already? She'd be the easiest for the killer to find.

David reached for her wrist, holding it so he could inspect the little pewter sun. "Let me take it, Ariel."

Her heart lurched at his suggestion. "What? Why?"

"I'll take it to a lab and have it checked out, see if there's anything special about it."

He could only understand the logical, so how could he ever really accept her? "David, what's special about this charm isn't something that can be measured in a laboratory."

"There are experts in this field, Ariel. Parapsychologists who can measure this kind of stuff."

Her mouth quirked into a smile. "This kind of stuff?" Her heart softened, touched by how hard he was trying to understand and help her.

A muscle ticked in his jaw. "I'm not sure what the technical terms are, but I can get in contact with one of these parapsychologists—"

She pressed her fingers against his lips. "I appreciate what you want to do," she said, "but until we catch this killer, I'm not taking off my charm."

His brown eyes darkened. "You don't need it, Ariel. *I* will keep you safe."

With the gun? She didn't voice the thought, didn't want to spoil the moment with the doubts that had had her eavesdropping at his locked office door.

"I don't know what I'd do without you," she told him. She'd lost Haylee, her job and any hope of reuniting with her family. She couldn't lose him, too. But what if he were only sticking with her out of chivalry, because he wanted to protect her?

"Shh," he said as he pressed a kiss against her lips.

Ariel wrapped her arms around his neck, clinging to him. If she couldn't emotionally hang on to him, she would physically until he pushed her away as her sister had.

"I'm not going anywhere," he promised her.

She managed a smile. "No, you're not," she agreed as she reached for the buttons on his shirt.

His deep voice vibrated with warning as he murmured her name. "Ariel…"

She was heedless of his threats as she pushed the shirt from his shoulders, baring his broad chest to her gaze and her touch. Her fingertips slid across his skin, his muscles rippling beneath. Then she tasted him, gliding her lips up his chest, where she nipped at his collarbone.

He groaned and his eyes squeezed shut as if in pain. Ariel could identify; she ached for him, too. His hands pushed up her skirt, his palms both rough and warm sliding along her thighs until he pushed them apart and stroked the heat of her through her thin cotton panties.

"David, I need you…*now*…."

Another lie. Even with passion burning in her veins, she lied. She didn't need him just *now,* she needed him *always*. She opened her mouth to tell him the truth, to accept his proposal, but all that escaped was a moan, as he pushed her panties aside and slid two fingers inside her. She arched her back, then lifted her sweater over her head. Her breasts bounced free, unbound by a bra, the nipples jutting toward him.

David answered their silent plea, tugging one into his mouth. His tongue laved the hard point while his fingers continued their sweet torture, sliding in and out of her.

Passion burned low in her belly as she trembled with the need for more even as the first climax crashed through her. With trembling hands she reached for him, unzipping his pants and pushing aside his boxers until he sprang free.

"Wait," he murmured, reaching into his wallet for a condom, always so logical and controlled even when flushed and shuddering with desire.

She suckled on his collarbone as he rolled on the latex. Then he lifted her onto his lap, driving into her, hot and hard.

"David!" She screamed his name, holding on tight to him as her world shattered. Again.

The mingled scents of lavender and sandalwood teased Ariel's nose, drawing her from a deep sleep. Before she fully awakened, she became aware of another sensation, of the links of her silver bracelet tugging at her wrist. Through cracked lids she spied David fumbling with her charm. Her heart shifted, thudding hard against her ribs. Fear kept her from sitting up in bed and demanding to know what the hell he was doing. Instead she murmured as if still asleep and rolled over, tucking her wrist beneath her.

Forcing her breathing to remain even and unaffected, she waited to see if he would try again for the charm. The mattress shifted as he moved, but he rolled away from her and slid his legs from under the satin sheets. With a soft thud his feet hit the floor.

Her fear dissipated, easing the burn in her lungs and slowing her rapid pulse. The charm held some fascination for him, probably because of what she'd told him. He couldn't have been trying to steal it. She reached out, but the smoke thickened, blocking her fingers from touching him.

Moonlight streaming through the windows painted his skin as golden a hue as his hair. The muscles in his back and arms rippled as he leaned over and pulled out the drawer of the nightstand. The light changed color, the gold turning to flame-orange as it glinted off the metal of the object he lifted from the drawer.

A gun.

Ty had come through on this favor, too. What did he owe David? What exactly was the history between them? She'd considered it none of her business before, something that had happened before her time and had nothing to do with her. Now she wondered….

The cords in his neck distended with tension as he stared down at the weapon in his hands. His breath shuddered out with such force that his shoulders shook.

Fear and doubt squeezed Ariel's heart, and her fingers, still extended toward him, curled back into a fist. She couldn't ask him all the questions churning in her mind. When he turned his head, she closed her eyes, feigning sleep.

She kept them closed as he moved around the room, clothing rustling as he dressed. She only opened them after the bedroom door closed behind him with a soft click. Then she slid across the satin sheets until she could reach the nightstand. The clock on top of the black lacquer table flashed two o'clock in luminous green. She cared less about the time than the contents of the drawer, but when she pulled it open, the gun was gone.

"Mama," Ariel called to her mother's ghost, who hovered in the smoke, her dark eyes wide with fear. "I need to hear you. I need you to tell me that David has nothing to do with the vendetta."

Her breath caught like a stabbing pain in her chest. "Please, Mama, tell me my doubts are unfounded."

Her mother's ghost said nothing, just faded away with the orange glow and the dissipating smoke. The only noise in the penthouse was the grind of the elevator as it descended to the lobby with David…and the gun.

* * *

Gates and guards. They thought that would keep them safe from him? They had no idea how powerful he was. Or how close.

Soon he would be even more powerful, once they were dead. But *they* had to find the youngest one yet, for him. Then he could reclaim the charms and kill them all, the last of the witches.

He pulled the hood over his head and stepped out of the vestibule. Candles blazed from the altar, pillars of smoke rising up from their flames to the rafters of the old church.

His church.

He was God to these people.

They knelt before the altar. They knelt before him, the dark robes hiding their bodies, the hoods their faces. They didn't laugh at him as the witches in his visions did. They worshipped him. They would do whatever he asked of them…and more.

Despite the concealing brown fabric, he knew the identity of each of them. He'd chosen them specifically, either because of bloodlines or a thirst for revenge. They shared a special bond, a common goal.

"We must protect ourselves from witchcraft," he declared, his voice echoing off the rafters and reverberating inside his head. His knees weakened, trembling a bit with the pain, but he couldn't give in to it.

He had to keep fighting. "We must destroy them before they manipulate our minds and steal our souls."

Or, more dangerous yet, their hearts.

"Beware their treachery. Stay the course. Remain strong." He spoke the warnings as much for himself as for the others. Maybe more.

The others began a chant, something he'd taught them in Latin about vanquishing witchcraft, about regaining power. *"Exstinguo…veneficus…"*

But the words ran together in his head with the throbbing pain. For a moment his vision blurred, and the witches appeared in the hooded robes. Their lips curved as they laughed at how they'd tricked him.

Rage whipped through him, and he swept an arm across the altar, knocking the candles over. Alarmed cries emanated from his followers. The flames caught the sleeve of his robe, but he pounded his arm against the altar, snuffing out the fire before the heat could sear his skin.

Then he glanced up, his eyes tearing as he tried to peer through smoke, an eerie orange light nearly blinding him. But he saw her.

The witch he'd burned—she hovered on the other side of the charred altar. Her mouth open, not in the scream last on her lips but in silent laughter.

She mocked him as she haunted him.

Chapter 10

Panting for breath, trembling with fear, Elena awoke alone, tangled in the sheets of her empty bed. Kirk, her husband, was gone again. A business trip, if she believed him. Somewhere else, if she trusted an earlier dream.

But if she trusted her dreams, any of them, she'd have to accept what Ariel had told her. The curse was real. The vendetta and her dreams—all those terrifying dreams of murder—were real. The ones she'd witnessed a while ago had already happened, if she believed her younger sister. Their aunts. Their mother. Hanged, crushed, burned…it had all really happened, just as she'd witnessed.

And the other one, of Ariel, it *would* happen, too.

Both her heart and her head aching, Elena doubled over from the pain. Seeing Ariel again had brought everything back to her—the guilt, the fear…it was tearing her apart. She squeezed her eyes shut, trying to blind herself to the vision reeling through her mind.

"Make it stop…." she murmured.

But the redhead kept running. The man, always hidden in the shadows, kept chasing her. Elena's heart hammered against her ribs, and sweat dribbled between her shoulder blades, as if she were the one running.

But she cowered, huddled in a heap in her bed. Ariel hadn't cowered or run, not in person. She'd been strong. Determined. And totally accepting of who and what she was.

A witch.

Elena shivered, the sweat chilling her skin. She couldn't accept what she was, what she could do. Not the way Ariel could. Guilt and regret churned in Elena's stomach, burning like acid. God, she'd been so horrible to her sister. But Ariel had caught her by surprise, not just by appearing out of nowhere but by being alive.

But how much longer could the redhead keep running before the man reached out of the shadows and caught her? Elena pushed her palms against her eyes, trying to blind herself to the vision. But it wouldn't matter. It wouldn't save Ariel. The man always caught her.

The little pewter charm that had been dangling from Ariel's wrist didn't protect her as she'd sworn it did. It was just a trinket. Nothing more. That was what Elena's grandmother had always said, but she didn't believe everything Thora told her.

In the darkness Elena fumbled beside her bed, dragging open the top drawer of the nightstand. Blindly she patted around inside, pushing aside handkerchiefs and a book, until her fingers grazed metal. Warm metal. She grasped the little pewter star so tightly that the points, even dull with age, dug into her flesh and heated her chilled skin.

She didn't wear it, as Ariel did, but she always kept it close. Maybe that was why she'd lied to her sister about losing it; she hadn't been about to hand it over to her. Hopefully it would protect Elena, because if the dreams were real, her sister was right—someone had resurrected the vendetta and started a witch hunt.

Lightning flashed, but the weather was calm and still outside. Through the partially open blinds the sky appeared clear. The lightning wasn't flashing there but inside Elena's head, illuminating the scene playing out in her mind. She couldn't fight it, not sleeping or awake. Again she panted for breath, as she had in her sleep. But she wasn't the one who'd been running. Now she knew the woman's identity for certain—it was Ariel, her long red hair streaming behind her as she struggled to outrun the arms reaching for her. Then the rope looped around her neck again.

Elena reached up, digging at her throat, trying to ease the tightness of the rough fibers against her skin. She sputtered for breath as she watched with her eyes open as her sister was dragged off her feet and lifted, the rope squeezing off her breath…until she gasped her last. Her mouth fell open on her last silent scream, her turquoise eyes rolling back inside her head.

Blinking furiously at tears, Elena finally saw the man, the one standing beside her sister's hanging body. At last he'd stepped out of the shadows. The lightning glinted off his golden hair and reflected like fire in his cold, dark eyes. He was the blond-haired man who'd been with Ariel. David Koster.

Elena's heart clenched as shock and fear gripped her. She had to warn her sister that the man she knew and apparently trusted was a killer. Her killer.

* * *

Despite Ariel's efforts, the killer had found her first. Or so Ariel assumed that was who had left her front door ajar and ransacked her house. Her heart beat fast and hard as she stepped into the living room, awash with sunlight streaming through the windows. Her sunny little house had been desecrated, papers strewn about the polished oak floor, her favorite chair slashed, its white stuffing protruding like tissue and bone from its jagged wound.

Who would do such a thing? She could think of only one—the person responsible for the deaths of her mother and aunts. Or was there someone else now, someone so determined to protect her reputation and position in society that she might threaten her sister to back off?

She shook her head, doubting that was Elena's style. No, she'd write a check instead, buy her silence.

Ariel wasn't about to keep quiet. She released a scream of frustration. She might have kicked or hit something, too, but the front door creaked behind her.

She doubted it was the killer returning to the scene of this petty crime. More likely it was Ty, continuing his favor to David by following her home from the Towers. But because she had learned to always be prepared, Ariel reached for her pepper spray, grasping the canister in a tight fist.

"You're not much of a housekeeper," a woman said, lifting her hands palm up when Ariel whirled on her.

"Elena!" Her sister's visit shocked her more than the break-in at her house. But Ariel smothered the spark of hope flaring to life in her heart. She couldn't handle much more disappointment. "Or should I call you Elle?"

The blonde's lips pulled into a tight line. "Only my grandmother calls me Elle."

From the bitterness hardening her sister's voice, Ariel doubted it was an affectionate nickname. "I still want to talk to her."

"Thora?" The icy blue eyes widened with alarm. "Why?"

Frustration simmered in Ariel again. Instead of releasing it in another scream, she crossed through the archway into her living room and knelt to pick up the papers strewn across the floor. "She might know something. Maybe she'll have an idea where Irina is."

"*I* will ask her," Elena said.

Ariel glanced up at her sister. "You'll help?" she asked doubtfully as her older sister hovered in the foyer between the open door and Ariel. She was almost outside now, she was so anxious to leave.

"Should you be touching anything?" Elena asked. "Shouldn't you wait until the police get here?"

Ariel shrugged. "I haven't called them."

"Someone broke into your house!"

Still clutching the papers, Ariel stood up and passed her sister to examine the door. "The jamb's not broken. Neither is the lock. Doesn't look like anyone broke in."

"So he had a key?" Elena asked, her breath audibly catching.

Ariel shook her head. "No. I must have left it unlocked." When she'd left in such a hurry to confront Thora Jones. "Only David and I have keys."

"David Koster?"

"Yeah, you saw him yesterday." The situation hadn't called for formal introductions. "You know, yesterday, when you wanted nothing to do with me. Why are you here now? Do you really want to help?"

Elena, clad in wool slacks and a silk shirt, both innocuous beige, stepped around Ariel onto the cement stoop that served as the front porch. Her gaze focused on her silver Lexus, she nodded. "Yes."

"Yesterday," Ariel said again, bitterness rising like acid in her throat, "you were willing to buy me off to get rid of me. What happened?"

Elena still wouldn't look at Ariel, just kept staring at her car as if planning a quick getaway. "I have dreams."

Somehow Ariel didn't think her sister was talking of goals or aspirations. "What about?"

Thin shoulders lifted and fell in a slight shrug. "Different things. Sometimes they're insignificant."

"And sometimes?"

Another shrug and a breathy reply. "They're not." She shuddered, then turned to Ariel, her blue eyes wide with fear. "But they *always* come true."

Ariel's heart beat hard again. "These aren't dreams, Elena. You have *visions*. Of the future. Like Mama had."

The icy blue eyes brightened with unshed tears. "No. I can't. I don't want this…."

"Gift," Ariel said with a derisive snort. She'd never gained anything with her ability; she'd only lost.

"Curse," Elena corrected her, her voice deep with bitterness.

Maybe it was better to see the past, what had already happened, than what was about to. Ariel had always been frustrated with helplessness that she was too late, that there was nothing she could have done to help. But to see the future and not know *how* to change it and be forced to wait for it to unfold…

"Tell me about your dreams, Elena."

Her older sister descended the couple of cement stairs to the driveway, obviously unwilling to speak of her visions. Usually the thick canopy of trees lining the road and Ariel's small yard cast shadows over the drive. But today a soft orange glow illuminated the area and Elena's car, where in the backseat a little girl, her blond curls mussed against the headrest of her booster seat, slept.

"You have a daughter!" *I have a niece.*

A smile full of mother's love and pride softened Elena's face, making her breathtakingly beautiful. "Stacia. She's four."

"I love kids," Ariel shared, wanting to open the back door and pull the little girl into her arms. But Elena stood between her daughter and her sister. Ariel didn't blame her; after all these years, they were strangers. "I'm a second grade teacher."

Elena nodded. "You were always good with Irina."

"So were you."

Elena sighed. "She was special, so sensitive she'd almost always know what you were thinking."

Ariel wished she knew what Elena was thinking now, what had her forehead puckered with worry, but then, she probably already knew. "We'll find Irina. If we work together. Did you dream of her?"

Elena shuddered. "Maybe. A while ago. But I'm not sure it was her. She had black curly hair like Mother's."

A sigh slipped from Ariel's lips. "It's been a long time since we saw her, and she was so young. The woman in your dream—what else did you notice about her?"

Elena's teeth nibbled her bottom lip a moment before she said anything more. When she spoke, her voice vibrated with fear, but not for herself. "She was dirty, unkempt. Wild-eyed, probably homeless."

Ariel's heart lurched. "I hope you're wrong."

"It's what I saw."

She spoke with such certainty, reminding Ariel of what she'd claimed when she'd first confessed to the dreams. "They always come true?"

Her teeth sunk deep enough in her lower lip to draw a thin bead of blood, Elena nodded.

"But that's good. She's alive. We know where to start looking." The streets. Alleys. Gutters. Tears burned Ariel's eyes, but she refused to be discouraged. Irina was alive. For now.

Her fingers clenched, crunching the papers she'd picked up from her floor and hadn't put away. She glanced down at the postcard, then held it out to Elena. "See the symbols. Of the charms. Mama circled them. We need to find Irina. We need to reunite. Then we can fight this killer."

Elena's chin dipped as she lowered her head. Her voice soft, she admitted, "I lied to you."

Ariel's heart lurched. "About the dreams?"

"About the charm." Elena reached into the pocket

of her beige slacks and pulled out the little pewter star. "I didn't lose it."

Ariel blew out a relieved breath. "Thank God. Hopefully Irina still has hers—"

"Take it," Elena said, holding her palm out toward her sister. "For protection."

Ariel glanced from the charm to the backseat where Elena's child slept, her head moving against the headrest as if she dreamd fitful dreams. "You keep it, to protect you and Stacia."

Ariel and her sisters weren't the last generation of Durikken/Cooper women. Stacia was.

"I think you need it more." Elena's delicate jaw tightened beneath her alabaster skin. "I dreamed about you, too."

Swallowing down a lump of fear, Ariel urged her, "Tell me about it."

The smoke rose from nowhere, and the orange light glowed, shining on Ariel, her sister and their mother's ghost as she rose up from the smoke. Elena's voice sounded distant, perhaps an echo of their dead mother's warning, as she described her dream. "It's dark. You're running."

Ariel was used to running—from her feelings, from her fears. "Am I running from someone?"

Elena nodded. "At first I couldn't see who. He was in the shadows, always in the shadows."

"You've had this dream more than once."

Again Elena nodded. "I told myself it was just a dream…until you came to the house yesterday."

"Now you know it's real, all of it. Our abilities. The vendetta."

"I've had other dreams. I saw a woman crushed by rocks. I saw another woman hanged." Her voice cracked, tears filling her eyes as she added, "I saw our mother burned."

Pain lanced through Ariel's heart. She squeezed her eyes shut to the image of their mother's ghost, to the horror and agony the woman had endured. "Oh, God, Elena…"

"Now do you know why I hate it? Why I don't want it to be real?"

Ariel nodded. "I know." She might be the only other person who did. "But we can use what you've seen to stop him. We can turn the curse into a blessing."

Elena shook her head, her eyes brimming with misery. "How?"

"Since you've seen them murdered, you've seen the killer. You can describe—"

"When those women died, I didn't see him. He was either in the shadows or wearing a brown robe with a hood that covered his head. Until last night…"

"When you had another dream." Ariel's stomach lurched. "You saw him kill someone else."

Elena nodded. "I saw him kill *you,* Ariel."

Everybody had to die sometime. But Ariel couldn't utter the flip remark and denigrate the special ability it had taken her sister twenty years to admit. Nor could she brush off the fear that had her trembling.

Elena continued, her voice a soft quaver, "He catches you. Then he hangs you, like he did the other woman."

"Marie." The name involuntarily slipped out, but it wasn't hers Ariel was interested in. It was *his.* "You saw him, Elena. You can describe him this time—"

"I don't need to," Elena interrupted. "I know who he is. So do you."

Dread pressed against Ariel's heart as she waited for her sister to reveal the killer's identity. Even though she braced herself, nothing could have prepared her for the name Elena uttered.

"The man who's going to kill you—it's David Koster."

She had followed the orange light, as she had to Armaya, but Ariel didn't know why it had led her here, to the worst area of Barrett, Michigan. Maybe there was a chance that her sister was right about Irina. But only about Irina...

Her heels scraped against the cracked cement as she hurried past old warehouses. Sheets of steel missing from the sides of the buildings exposed their interiors, empty but for old crates and other debris. The steel that remained on roofs and walls was discolored with rust and age, the properties long abandoned. Like the people who lived down here.

Despite the warm spring air, she shivered, her heart aching with the thought of her baby sister living on the streets. Elena had to be wrong…about *everything*.

David would *never* hurt Ariel. He loved her. His love burned in his eyes every time he took her in his arms. When he moved over her, joining their bodies together, possessing her.

She closed her eyes, and the image of him leaning over the gun sprang to her mind. Had he been about to use that gun on her? Where had he gone in the middle of the night?

She hadn't heard from him yet. Not that she'd called him. She couldn't.

Fingers clutched at her sleeve, startling Ariel into reaching for the pepper spray canister she'd tucked in a pocket. "What—"

"Miss," a voice rasped, the person's sex indistinguishable under his or her baggy clothes and stocking cap. The west Michigan spring weather warranted Ariel's light sweater but not the heavy jacket, scarf and hat this person wore. For warmth or for disguise?

She grasped the canister tightly. "Yes?"

"You're looking for someone? A woman?"

Ariel's pulse kicked, racing with excitement. She'd been able to ask only a few people, those who hadn't scurried away in fear of a stranger, if they'd seen Irina. Not that anyone would know her name—Irina might not even know that if it had been changed after her adoption. "Yes. She's about twenty-four, twenty-five. Her hair is dark and might be long and curly. And she has big, dark eyes."

The person nodded. "Sounds like the Gypsy girl."

Hope jumped in Ariel's heart. "You've seen her?"

"I think she was around here…a while ago…."

"Where?"

"A block or so down," the person said. "Near the old church."

Irina would have taken sanctuary there. Above the warehouses, the old steeple was just visible, the bell dangling drunkenly from only a couple ropes. Could she be this close to finding her little sister?

Ariel reached into her other pocket, pulling out a folded bill, grateful for the information. But when she turned back toward the informant, the person rushed away, surprisingly quick despite the weight and confinement of all his clothes. A warning bell clanged in Ariel's head.

This was too easy, and nothing in Ariel's life had ever been too easy, only too good to be true. Was that the case with David? She drew in a deep breath, forcing the nerves and doubts away. She couldn't fall prey to either.

Even suspecting it could be a trap, Ariel hurried toward the church, the steeple her visual guide. As she drew closer, though, her steps slowed. Warehouses flanked both sides of the old church, everything boarded up and deserted. No one around to hear her scream.

The perfect trap. But she had to check it out. It was the only lead on Irina that they'd had. They. She and David. Elena had either misinterpreted her dream or she'd lied. She couldn't be right....

Tears blurred her vision as Elena's warning repeated itself in her head. *The man who's going to kill you—it's David Koster.*

The smoke rolled in, further blinding her with its thickness and the eerie glow of the orange light. *Mama, help me!*

But no ghost appeared, just the smoke and light. And the faint odor of sandalwood and lavender. *Mama...*

Ariel glanced around, but the streets were empty.

Only an old liquor bottle rolled across the sidewalk, breaking as it struck the gutter. Not able to back out now, when she might be so close to Irina, Ariel crossed the street, stepping over the broken bottle. She climbed the cracked concrete stairs to the arched doors of the church. Graffiti covered the old wood panels, insignias of gangs and foreign words. A rusted chain, clasped with an old padlock, wound through the door handles, holding them closed.

She grasped the handles, yanking on them. The hinges creaked and groaned as the old doors shuddered in the jambs. "Hello? Is anyone in there?"

Her voice echoed eerily, as if it had somehow filtered into the empty church. Then she noticed the board next to the doors. Instead of being nailed over the broken window, it just leaned against the bottom half of the stained-glass arch. With trembling fingers she lifted the wood away. The opening was big enough for her to squeeze through, the jagged edges of broken glass catching at her jeans and sweater as she passed between them.

"Is anyone here?" she called again, her voice reverberating off the high rafters in the domed ceiling.

But suddenly she wasn't alone, as smoke encircled the altar. Her mother hovered above it, her arms flailing. Waving Ariel away or closer?

Her heels clicked against worn marble as she

followed the aisle past the pews toward the front. Someone had been inside recently. Charred wicks lay in pools of wax, the candles burned so low that the altar must have caught fire. The old pine surface bore the black scars of flames. Ariel's breath caught, her lungs hurting. In the charred wood someone had carved three symbols. A star, a sun and a crescent moon.

Fear coursing through Ariel, she reached for the charm dangling from wrist, holding it tight between her fingertips. Warmth and comfort spread up her arm, through her body, dispelling the fear.

Then someone called out her name, the voice sharp with warning. "Ariel!"

Alarmed, she turned, catching a glancing blow of metal, cold and hard, against her temple. Her knees buckled, and she fell to the floor beside the altar.

Chapter 11

Dirt from the floor ground against the skin of Ariel's cheek. She blinked hard, nearly succumbing to unconsciousness until the same anxious feminine voice called her name again. "Ariel!"

The smoke thickened, the orange glow shining warmly against her prone body. "Mama…"

She could finally hear ghosts…maybe because she was about to become one?

Then someone else called her name. "Ariel!"

Banging echoed loud inside the church as the doors rattled back and forth under the force of fists or something else hammering at them. Then closer, footsteps vibrated against the floor, and someone passed Ariel. She glimpsed black shoes and the hem of a brown robe as the person rushed past her to the vestibule behind the altar.

She planted her palms and pushed up, swaying dizzily for a moment before regaining her balance. She started toward the vestibule when strong fingers closed around her arm.

"Ariel, are you all right?"

She turned to Ty. "I'm fine." Because of the charm and her mother's warning. Without their protection, she suspected she'd have been hit harder. Or, worse, she'd be dead. "Did you see him?"

"Who?" Ty asked. "I lost you a while back when you stopped to talk to some homeless guy. What the hell are you doing down here, Ariel? Trying to get yourself killed?"

"I thought I had a lead on Irina."

"From who? The homeless guy? They'll tell you anything for a buck," he scoffed.

He was probably right, but she hadn't paid the guy. Someone else had, to steer her to the church. She glanced behind her, to the symbols carved into the altar. Instead of showing them to Ty, she shook her head, wincing as her temple throbbed.

"You're hurt," he said, touching her face where

blood oozed from a shallow cut. "What happened? Did someone attack you?"

The lies came so easily now, she let another one roll off her tongue. "I must have tripped and fallen."

Ty was David's friend. Could she trust him? Could she trust either of them?

She was still asking herself that question when, later, he paced her living room, stopping to examine the torn drapes and slashed furniture. "When did this happen?" he asked.

She shrugged, nearly dislodging the ice pack pressed against her temple. The swelling was minor, the wound already scabbed over. She'd been lucky—no, she'd been blessed. "Last night."

"You were with David?"

Part of the night, until he'd left with the gun. She nodded, wincing as the ice pack scraped against her cut, so she tossed it in the trash. "The door was open when I came home this morning, and I found it like this." She gestured toward the mess.

"And you didn't call anyone? Not David? Or me? Or the police?" He stopped in front of her, his navy gaze intent on her face. "What's going on, Ariel?"

"You tell me. You've been following me," she reminded him.

"Now I see why David asked me to. You need a keeper!" He shoved a slightly shaking hand through his hair, grasping the short, dark strands, perhaps trying to hold on to his temper. "I didn't come by here until late this morning. Some blonde was just pulling away in a Lexus."

Her eyes narrowed at his vagueness. "You ran the plate. You know her name."

"Elena Jones-Phillips."

"She's my sister, Ty."

Surprise cracked his voice. "You found one of them?"

"By accident," she admitted, accepting that she was no sleuth or she would have listened to her sixth sense when it told her not to enter that church. "David didn't tell you?"

"I haven't talked to David all day."

Neither had she. "Maybe you're following the wrong person," she remarked, her heart beating hard as her doubts and suspicions returned. She'd suspected he'd been keeping something from her. But what Elena claimed…

He lowered his gaze, saying nothing.

"You don't know what he's up to either," she said, dread tying her stomach into knots. And because he was unaware of David's actions, maybe she could trust Ty, as much as she was able to trust anyone. She needed to talk to someone. "You shouldn't have given him the gun."

His gaze lifted to hers. "You know about the gun?"

She nodded. "He took it and went somewhere in the middle of the night. And neither of us has heard from him since."

"I'm sure he'll have a reasonable explanation," Ty insisted loyally.

"He always does," she agreed. "Like for following me. He was doing that before he asked you to. But it was by accident. He just happened upon my leaving for Armaya the first time. The second time he beat me there."

"What are you saying?" Ty wanted to know.

She blew out a ragged breath. "It's what my sister said."

"She knows about all that?"

"She only knows what she *sees*."

Ty lifted his scarred brow. "She sees stuff like you do?"

"No, not exactly. She sees things *before* they happen. She actually has a chance of helping people who might get hurt. That's why she came here this morning—to warn me."

He glanced around the ransacked room. "I'd say she was a little late."

Ariel's smiled halfheartedly. "For this. But I'm still alive."

His blue eyes widened. "Ariel…" Then, as if

gathering information from witnesses, he directed her, "Just tell me what she said, what she saw...about you."

Not knowing how else to say it, she just blurted it out. "My murder."

All the color drained from Ty's face, as if he'd seen a ghost. But she wasn't dead yet. He drew her into a loose embrace. "She's wrong! That's not going to happen. We're going to keep you safe. David's making sure of it. That's why he wanted the gun, to protect you."

She squeezed her eyes shut, not able to look at Ty when she told him, "She thinks it's David."

"What?" Ty asked in disbelief.

She didn't want to believe what her sister had said either, but she had to share Elena's accusation with someone, someone who knew David better than Ariel did. "She thinks David is the one who's going to kill me."

"She's crazy, Ariel, or she's lying!"

That had been Ariel's first reaction. She'd screamed *liar* so loudly at her sister that Stacia had stirred in the backseat. Then, unwilling to hear another bad word about David, Ariel had whirled away and gone back into her violated house. Her sister hadn't followed to defend or explain herself, leaving Ariel alone with her questions and doubts.

"Why would she lie? What can she gain from breaking up me and David?" Ariel wondered aloud. That question nagged at her even though she dismissed what Elena had said.

Ty shrugged, his shoulders jerking beneath the dark T-shirt he wore. "I don't know. And you don't know *her*, Ariel. It's been twenty years. She's not the little girl you remember."

"She's a cold, bitter woman," Ariel admitted.

"She's the one who wants to hurt you," Ty insisted. "I know David loves you. If he didn't…" His fingers tightened on her shoulders. "But he does."

"I don't want to believe that David would ever hurt me." She had struggled to suppress her doubts for so long, but now all of them spilled out. "But he was there when we found my aunt, the one covered in rocks. I saw him removing them, but…"

"You think he could have been putting them on?"

"I know that's crazy, that he'd never hurt anyone. He's so kind. So generous. You know him, Ty. You have history," she reminded him.

Ty nodded. "Yes, we do. I grew up with David, even lived with him and his folks for a while."

"After your dad died. He told me that."

"Did he tell you *how* my dad died?" Ty asked, his voice low.

Ariel shook her head. "I just assumed an accident or illness."

"He was killed," Ty informed her dispassionately, as if he didn't care. Since it had been so long ago, maybe he didn't anymore. Or maybe he never had.

"I'm sorry, Ty."

"He wasn't the kind of man anyone would mourn, least of all me," he said bitterly. "If he hadn't died, he probably would have killed me…if not that day, another day."

Something about his tone, about the guilt tingeing his words, had her asking, "Did you kill him, Ty?" Then she rushed to add, "If you did, it was self-defense. You can't hang on to any guilt over it. You had to have been just a kid." Or he wouldn't have lived with David's parents. He would have been out on his own, as she'd been the minute she turned eighteen.

"*I* didn't kill him, Ariel."

She blew out a little relieved breath.

"David did."

Her heart skipped a beat, then resumed at a mad pace. "David?"

"He saved my life," Ty insisted. "The old man was beating me, like he did pretty much every day. Even before I told him, David had figured out what Dad was doing and he wanted to protect me." His mouth tipped up into his lopsided smile. "But he was just a kid, too."

"How old was he?"

"Eleven. And until we were teenagers, David was pretty scrawny," he said. "He knew he couldn't physically threaten my dad, so he borrowed his dad's service revolver. Mike Koster was a cop."

Like Ty.

"David waited until his dad fell asleep, then he took the gun and brought it to my house and walked in on one of my beatings." He paused as if unsure he should continue. "He pointed it at the old man and told him to stop."

"He didn't stop," Ariel surmised.

Ty shook his head. "No, he laughed at David and reached for him. I don't know if David got scared and fired or the old man inadvertently pulled the trigger himself when he grabbed it. Either way, it was an accident."

She couldn't imagine the emotional scars killing someone would leave for an adult, let alone a child. "He never told me…."

"He doesn't tell anyone. His record was expunged, but still he worries that someone will find out."

"That's why he avoids the media," she realized, much of David's behavior becoming clear.

Ty nodded. "I don't think there's any way

someone could find out, or they would have by now.
A lot of articles have been done about David, but he's
convinced that it would take only one determined
reporter…" And David's secret would be revealed.

"Why did you tell me?" Ariel asked. "To warn
me?"

A ragged breath escaped Ty's lips. "No. I wanted
you to know that David will do anything to protect
someone he cares about. It took him a lot to ask me
for that gun, Ariel. After what happened, he hates
them so much he wouldn't even consider becoming
a cop. He broke the family tradition—he and his dad
hardly talk anymore because of it."

Or because he'd killed someone with his dad's
gun? Maybe Ty had meant to calm her fears, but all
Ariel could think was that if David had killed
before, he could kill again, even if Ty's dad's death
was an accident. "I don't know…."

"Then ask him."

Ariel snorted. "How?" she asked, "So, David,
before I accept your proposal I need to know something. Are you a killer?"

"If you have to ask, I'd suggest you say no,"
David advised, as he strode through the archway
into the living room.

Conflicting emotions waged an internal battle in
Ariel: relief that he was all right, that whatever had

drawn him out in the middle of the night with a gun hadn't caused him harm, and fear, as much because he'd overheard her doubts as from the doubts themselves. "David…"

Ty cleared his throat. "I'll leave you two alone."

"Are you sure?" David asked not his friend but her, his eyes dark with bitterness and pain. "Maybe you're scared to be alone with me."

She wouldn't be alone. Sweetly scented smoke filtered into the room, glowing orange. While she couldn't see her mother yet, she knew she was close, as she'd been at the church. Trying to protect her, to warn her…about David?

Ariel shivered, remembering the voice calling her name earlier that day. It had to have been Mama, warning her of danger, keeping her conscious, saving her from a killer. Perhaps just finding Elena and seeing her charm had strengthened Ariel's ability.

So she would be safe with David. If she wasn't, her mother would be warning her. But it wasn't her mother's presence that reassured her, it was David's. Her doubts weakened by her love for him.

Ty lifted his scarred eyebrow, asking, "Do you want me to stay?"

She shook her head. "I'll be fine." Even if David decided he couldn't be with a woman who could even think he might be a killer. A broken heart wasn't life-threatening; if it was, she'd have died years ago.

As he walked past his friend on the way to the door, Ty whispered, "I'm sorry."

David didn't even look at him, his gaze intent on Ariel. He didn't speak again until they were alone. "So the killer thing... Ty told you."

"Someone had to," she pointed out, inwardly breathing a sigh of relief that he may not have caught on to her doubts. "You were never going to tell me."

"No, I wasn't," he agreed. "I didn't want you looking at me the way you are now," he said, his deep voice quiet. "Probably the same way you didn't want me looking at you." He expelled a ragged breath. "With fear in your eyes, like I'm damaged or crazy."

"David," she said, softening her voice with understanding, "it was an accident. You were only eleven years old."

"I was old enough to know what I was doing when I took my father's gun," he insisted.

"Yes—saving the life of your best friend."

"I don't know that. I don't know if he would have ever actually killed Ty." He scrubbed his hands over his face. "And I've been living with that since I was eleven."

"Look at Haylee's father, what he did."

He shrugged, his broad shoulders bowing with the burden he'd carried for so long. "But he wasn't Ty's dad. I don't know if I did the right thing, and I will never know."

"David, it was an accident—"

"Actually, the authorities called it involuntary manslaughter since I brought the gun there. I knew what I was doing was wrong." His dark eyes swirled with emotion, revealing a hint of his tortured soul. "Bringing that *gun*…" He shuddered, as if the thought of one filled him with dread. "Pointing it at him…"

"You were protecting your friend." And he'd asked Ty for a gun to protect her, despite how much he hated them. The last of her doubts receded, leaving only guilt that she'd ever had any.

"I'm not sure my parents thought that. They never looked at me the same after that day," he shared. "Even though I only got probation, I think they might have been happier if I'd gone away for a while. I think they always worried that I'd done it on purpose. That I *am* a killer."

"David!"

His deep voice so cold, he reminded her, "I heard your question. You have that fear now, too. That's why I didn't want you to know. I couldn't stand it if you were frightened of me."

She couldn't deny that she sometimes feared

him, but maybe she was more afraid of how vulnerable loving him made her. Perhaps her doubts had been just another way to push him away, to protect herself from falling even harder for him.

"I'm scared of how much I love you," she admitted. So much that she could be risking her life just being alone with him…if her sister's vision were true. But love, real love, was worth any risk. She realized that now, maybe too late.

No sympathy softened his voice when he replied, "Then you know how I feel."

"I've never felt like this before," she said. So in love that nothing else mattered, not even her own safety. "I don't know how to handle a relationship like ours. I'm feeling my way in the dark here. I need you to hold my hand, to help me find my way."

He ignored her outstretched hand. "It's only dark because you don't trust me, Ariel."

"I do…." Maybe that wasn't entirely true, but she wanted to trust him. She just didn't know how; she hadn't trusted anyone in twenty years.

"No, Ariel," he said, shaking his head. "If you trusted me, you wouldn't keep pushing me away."

She winced, unable to deny his allegation without lying to him. Between the two of them, there had been enough false truths and honest lies, whether real or of omission. "David…"

"What's going on?" he asked, gesturing around her ransacked house. "Do you think I did this?"

She hadn't until Elena had reminded her that he was the only other one with a key. "The door wasn't forced—"

"*Why* would I do this?" he asked, throwing up his hands as if ready to concede defeat.

She lifted her chin, willing to fight for them even if he wasn't. But she couldn't fight what she didn't know; neither of them could. "Maybe you were trying to find out if I'm keeping any other secrets."

"Are you?"

She drew in a quick breath. "Elena came to see me today."

"That's great," he said, his deep voice softening, "especially after how cold she was to you yesterday."

As she had with Ty, Ariel just blurted out what Elena had told her. "Yeah, well, having a vision of my death thawed her out."

"Ariel!" His hands shook as he grabbed her shoulders, pulling her close to him. Tension radiated from his long, hard body. "She's just trying to scare you—"

"Well, it worked," she wasn't too proud to admit as she jerked away from him. She had to be strong enough to tell him the rest—and she wouldn't be if she melted in his arms.

"What did she tell you?" he asked, anger darkening his eyes.

Ariel inhaled deeply again, breathing in the comforting scent of lavender and sandalwood. But still her mother's ghost had not visually appeared.

"Ariel, tell me what she said," he demanded, impatience sharpening his voice as he reached for her again.

"Apparently I get hanged, like Marie," she said, forcing nonchalance even as her heart hammered with nerves and fear.

"Oh, my God!"

She bit her lip but couldn't hold back the rest of her admission. "And apparently you're the one who hangs me."

"That's crazy!" His dark eyes widened as he realized what she was thinking. "Oh, my God, you…believe…her."

Her heart clenched almost as if she could feel his pain. "David…"

He dropped his hands from her and stepped away. "You actually believe that I could hurt you."

"I don't!" she insisted weakly, for she had considered the possibility more than once.

"So you think I'm responsible for what happened to your aunts. You think I'm a *killer!*" Because he was, because he had killed even though by accident, he had to be even more sensitive to that description.

"David, no…" The tears wouldn't stop now; they flowed in torrents as sobs strangled her. "Please… listen to me. I didn't, not—"

"Not really? Just a little bit?" His mouth twisted into a hard, bitter line. "Well, that's better then."

"I know you're hurt," she said, her voice cracking along with her heart. "I would *never* hurt you on purpose."

"I would never hurt you, either, Ariel," he promised her. "Too bad you don't trust me enough to know that."

"David—"

"No, you actually don't trust me at all. Your sister, she's a stranger to you, but you believe her over me, over my love for you." She glimpsed the tear shining on his face as it streaked down his cheek and clung to the edge of his square jaw. His dark eyes cold, he told her, "Don't bother returning the ring. I don't want it back."

He turned away, his feet hitting the floor with such force that it vibrated.

"David!"

The door slammed behind him.

Ariel sank to the floor on her knees, wrapping her arms around herself to hold in the pain. "Mama," she called, but her mother's ghost didn't appear. Nor did Haylee's.

Like most of her life, Ariel had no one to offer her comfort. She was all alone again.

Chapter 12

Mist swirled around the merry-go-round and swing set, light sparkling on the monkey bars where little hands had worn the paint off the metal. Haylee sat in the one of the swings, pumping it with her legs so that it swayed high and low, like Ariel's emotions.

Maybe that was why the ghost of the little girl had returned; she'd felt Ariel's pain and knew she was needed to comfort and soothe.

But no one could do that now. No one but David. Ariel glanced down at his ring. Despite what he'd told her, she should have given it back. He didn't want to be with her anymore. And she didn't trust him. She wished she could, but trust wasn't easy for her to give, maybe impossible. After he'd left her, she'd even checked his background, seeing if she could trace his heritage back to any McGregors. She hadn't found any. But then, she hadn't been able to trace back three hundred and fifty years.

"I'll go play with her," a soft voice said, as a little girl and her mother walked onto the playground.

"Who?" the mother asked.

"The girl on the swings."

"But no one's there."

Ariel turned around to face her sister and her niece. Her niece who could see what Ariel saw. Stacia looked up at her, those blue eyes bright and intelligent, and Ariel realized that maybe she saw *more*.

Did Elena know?

"She's gone, Mommy," Stacia said with a little sigh of disappointment.

Ariel glanced back over her shoulder, where the swing rocked back and forth even though it was empty now, Haylee, the mist and the light gone.

"Was there someone there?" Elena asked, her eyes anxious.

Ariel nodded, but she didn't tell her sister that the child had been a ghost. She didn't think Elena was ready to accept that her daughter was like them.

She'd barely been able to accept that her dreams were real, that they were visions of the future. From the dark circles bruising the alabaster skin beneath her eerie eyes, Elena still struggled with acceptance.

"Why did you want to see me?" Elena asked after her daughter had hopped onto a swing and started it moving, her legs pumping as Haylee's had.

"I need to talk to you."

"Why?" Elena asked, bitterness adding even more of a chill to her imperious voice. Unlike Ariel, who wore jeans and a sweatshirt, Elena had dressed up even for a playground meeting. She wore a linen skirt with a blue silk blouse and high-heeled pumps, which sunk into the sand and wood chips. "You don't believe what I tell you."

"Why should I?" More importantly, why *had* she? Why had she been so willing to doubt David? That wasn't a question her sister could answer, though. "I don't know you. You lied to me the first time we met, claiming you didn't have the charm. I have no reason to trust *you*."

Elena bowed her head, her blue gaze sliding away from Ariel's. "You blame me for what happened twenty years ago, for us getting taken away from Mother."

"Not at all," Ariel assured her, realizing David had been right about Elena feeling guilty. "We were just kids. We had no control over…anything. And I'm sure your grandmother did what she thought was best for you."

Under her breath Elena muttered, "I'm not so sure about that." Then, raising her voice, she asked again, "If you don't trust me, why do you want to talk to me?"

"I have no reason to believe you, but still you put doubts in my head," Ariel admitted, guilt flashing through her over how badly she'd hurt David.

"You must have already had some."

She bit her lip. "I shouldn't have, no matter what you *saw*. I love David."

"It's as easy to love the wrong man as the right," Elena said, obviously from a bitter place of experience.

"David isn't the wrong man." But he might never forgive her for her lack of trust; that had hurt him more than her lies.

"Then you're still together." She gestured to the ring on Ariel's finger.

She sighed. "I don't know *what* we are."

"You're alive. That's the important thing. You can love again," her older sister promised her. "You can't live again."

Ariel wasn't so sure about that, and her sister's comments raised some suspicions about the state of her marriage. Maybe because of the curse, a happily ever after wasn't possible for Durikken descendants. But Ariel was sick of running from the possibility of rejection and pain. She wanted to try with David. She really needed to talk to him more than she needed to speak with Elena.

She drew in a deep breath, bracing herself. "I need you to tell me *exactly* what you saw in your dream."

Elena closed her eyes, obviously reluctant to relive her vision. "God, Ariel…"

"Tell me!"

Her sharp tone drew a glance from Stacia. "Mommy?"

"I'm fine, honey," Elena assured her, her heels sinking into the sand as she stepped farther back from the swing set. She lowered her voice and turned on Ariel. "This isn't the time or the place—"

"You can't drop a bombshell on me like you did and leave it at that. I need the details."

Elena blew out a shaky breath. "I already told you, you're running—"

"Where am I?"

Elena shrugged. "I don't know. It's dark. I can't see the building."

"You know I'm inside somewhere then? I'm not out on the street."

"I guess."

Ariel sucked in a quick breath as her heart kicked against her ribs. "And you see David chasing me?"

Elena's teeth nibbled at her lip. "I don't actually see him chase you. He's still in the shadows then."

"When do you see him?"

"After the noose has been put around your neck, after you're pulled up to the rafters."

Ariel swallowed hard, her throat burning as if she felt the rope digging into her skin, cutting off her breath. "Do you see David pulling me up?"

Elena shook her head. "I don't see his face until you're hanging, until after you're dead."

Relief filled Ariel. "You don't understand your vision," she accused her sister. "You don't see David killing me, you see him *finding* me."

"But he's there, Ariel, right as you're dying."

Ariel nodded. "Of course. He's trying to protect me, trying to save me."

"But he doesn't," Elena pointed out in a soft whisper. "You die."

Now Ariel shook her head, dismissing the vision. "That's not going to happen. We'll stop this killer." Who wasn't David. "To do that, we have to find our little sister. Now."

Suddenly smoke rose, enveloping the playground. In the middle, under the orange glow, her mother's ghost hovered, her head nodding approval and she whispered, "Yes."

Tears burned Ariel's eyes with relief. She could *hear* her; it had been her mother's voice back at the church.

Elena lifted her hands palm up. "I don't know how to help. I don't know anything about Irina."

"But you dreamed about her, that she looked as if she lived on the streets."

"But I don't know if it was *her.* She was only four years old when we were split up. I have no idea what she would look like now as an adult."

"Then how did you know I was the woman you saw in your vision?" Ariel asked, growing frustrated with Elena's inability to understand her gift. If only her sister would stop fighting it and accept it…as Ariel finally had. She only hoped it didn't take a brush with the killer before Elena accepted it.

Her older sister reached out, wrapping one of Ariel's red tresses around her finger. "This. You're distinctive."

"Like you." With Elena's pale blond hair and icy blue eyes, it was hard to believe she had an ounce of their mother's Gypsy blood.

"Irina looked like our mother—like all of the Durikken women—so I don't know if I'm seeing her or one of them. An aunt, a cousin." She sighed. "I just don't know...."

"It has to be her," Ariel insisted. "There is no one else. Just you, me and..." She gestured toward where her niece swung back and forth. Her little legs didn't pump now; it was as if someone pushed her. Maybe her grandmother, who hovered protectively near her.

Elena bit her lip as her gaze focused on her daughter. She blinked hard, as if holding back tears. In sympathy, Ariel reached out, but before she could put her arm around her sister, Elena stepped away and asked, "Have you seen Irina? You know, her...?"

"Ghost?" Ariel shook her head, hurting inside at another familial rejection. "No." And she didn't believe that homeless person had, either. "If I had, it would be too late."

Elena expelled a ragged sigh of relief. "So she's still alive."

"For now," Ariel agreed, but she couldn't be sure. As she'd realized earlier, if Irina had forgotten them, her ghost probably wouldn't know to seek out Ariel, either. Ariel would have to find her, as she had her aunts.

"I don't know what you want me to do," Elena said. "I can't just make myself dream about her. This...curse...doesn't work that way."

"Gift," Ariel corrected her, defending their heritage despite all the times she'd considered it a curse, too. She couldn't be certain of when she'd finally accepted it—before or after she'd fallen to the floor of the church, where she might have died if not for her dead mother's warning. "It is a gift."

"You really feel that way about seeing ghosts?" Elena asked, her blue eyes filled with doubt.

"I didn't used to," she admitted. Elena might be unable to offer affection, but at least she could sympathize. The tight feeling in her chest that had haunted Ariel for the past twenty years eased a bit. "I couldn't hear them."

"They didn't talk to you?"

"They would try," Ariel admitted, "but I couldn't hear them. I'd see their mouths move and I'd know they were trying to communicate, but—"

"'You need to learn to listen, Ariel,'" Elena said with an affected lilting accent.

A smile tipped up Ariel's lips at the corners. "Mama…"

"I never understood why she told you that," Elena mused. "You were always the obedient one. I was…"

"Not," Ariel remembered, her lips twitching into a bigger smile. "I never told her, but she must have known what gift I had."

"Curse," Elena insisted. "We're all cursed."

When they were kids, there had been no arguing with Elena, so Ariel abandoned the curse/gift debate and concentrated on what was most important to her. "But after finding you, I began to hear Mama." She didn't tell her where, sparing her the circumstances. "Finding you—the other charm—must have increased my ability. That's why we have to find Irina. I know that if we're reunited and the charms are, too…"

Elena shook her head, her blue eyes soft. "Don't get your hopes up. She was so young. There's no guarantee she managed to hang on to the charm."

"I know we need all the charms." As if in confirmation, the orange glow encircled Ariel, Elena and Stacia.

She needed to return to the church where she'd found symbols of the charms carved into the charred altar. But she couldn't ask Elena to come along; she couldn't put her at risk when her sister had a child depending on her.

Ariel knew how much it hurt to lose her mother. She didn't want her niece to suffer that same loss. "You have your charm?" she asked Elena. "You're wearing it?"

Her sister shook her head, the blond hair brushing across her shoulders. "I never wear it. *I can't.*"

"But it'll keep you safe—"

"It might keep *you* safe, but it would put *me* in more danger," Elena admitted, her voice cracking with emotion she somehow kept from her icy eyes.

"Elena, if you're in danger, let me help you—"

"Don't worry about me. I'll be fine." The imperious chill entered her sister's voice again, dismissing Ariel even though she stood by her side.

Ariel realized she had only one person she could count on besides herself. Or she'd had him, before her suspicions had pushed him away.

Through eyes squinted with pain, he watched them from the woods, the two witches. And what about the little girl? Was she one, too? Probably.

He could take them all out at once. As he anticipated the kill, his nails dug into the bark of the tree behind which he hid. A pond sparkled in the sun, just beyond the playground where the women stood. He could drown them all. The killings had to be ritualistic or he wouldn't inherit their power. Eli had written that in the journal. Even though the book was illegible now, *he* would always remember the words in it, the directions on how to conduct a witch hunt.

But to take on all of them at once? His nails dug deeper, drawing blood to seep into the bark. He hated the quickening of his pulse, hated that it was fear coursing through his veins. Fear of their power.

The three of them combined could overcome what he'd gained. What he knew. They could don those hooded robes; they could set him afire, the way he'd burned their mother.

He could see her now, dancing on the smoke rolling through the woods, taunting him. He'd killed her, but she wouldn't stay dead. She wouldn't go away.

He had to kill them all before she'd leave. But he had to kill them…one at a time. He had waited long enough for them to lead him to the youngest sister. He would just have to find her himself. But he was getting weaker; he needed the power of at least one charm.

And the redheaded one had to go first. To him, she was the most dangerous, the one who could beguile him with her beauty. Maybe her sun charm would be enough to make him stronger, at least strong enough to get the charms from the other two. Then they would have to die, too—he couldn't leave any witches alive.

Chapter 13

Even though hers was the only image the mirrors reflected back, Ariel didn't ride the elevator to David's penthouse alone. Ghosts accompanied her. Of her mother. Of her aunts.

She closed her eyes to the thick mixture of smoke and mist, to the kaleidoscope of light and ethereal faces. Again she considered herself more fortunate than Elena. She could shut out the ghosts. If she ignored them long enough, they'd go away. Elena couldn't fight her visions.

Maybe that was what Ariel had been doing all along, why she hadn't been able to hear the ghosts—because subconsciously she'd been afraid of what they might say. Tonight she was afraid even to look at them. She didn't want them raising her doubts again, undermining the trust she was trying so hard to give to David.

She kept her eyes closed until the elevator stopped. When she opened them, she was completely alone, only the foyer of the penthouse stretching before her. No lights shone from the living room, so she backtracked for the stairs. She met him in the hall as he stepped out of his den. Before she could glimpse the inside, he pulled the door closed, but no lock clicked. That, like so many other things, she'd let her mistrust distort.

Like his love. Only there was no love in his eyes as he stared at her, his gaze empty and hard. "If you're here to give the ring back, I don't want it," he told her, his voice roughened by emotion.

"I'm not here to return your ring," she said, her intention to wear it always, first as his fiancée, then as his wife—if he could forgive her. "I'm here to explain myself, if you'll listen."

"What's to explain?" he scoffed. "You think I'm a killer."

"David, you have to admit you've done things that have raised my doubts. You followed me—"

"I told you why. You were dodging me. I came

by to check on you and you were pulling out of the driveway. If you hadn't already taken off once after Haylee's death, I wouldn't have followed you."

Pride lifted her chin—it was another of her defense mechanisms, like anger. "So it's my fault?"

"You keep pushing me away, Ariel. I can't take it anymore."

"Whether you believe me or not about the witch hunt, someone's after me, David. Someone's killing my family. I have a right to be as scared and paranoid as I want. I'd be a fool if I wasn't." And Ariel was nobody's fool. She wouldn't apologize for protecting herself. She spun toward the stairs, but he grabbed her, his hand tight around her wrist, pressing the sun charm into her skin.

"I'm the fool, Ariel. Forgive me."

"Forgive you? Why?" He'd done nothing except be there for her, loving her. Remorse filled her, vanquishing her anger and pride. "I'm sorry, David. I never should have doubted you."

"But you're right. You had every reason to run and keep me—anyone—at a distance. You're scared."

Her fear had always been more for her heart than her life, though. She reached for him, brave enough to risk rejection, to fight for her happiness. Her arms closed around his waist, his body warm and hard against hers.

"I need you, Ariel," he confessed, his voice thick with emotion. "God, I've missed you."

"It's only been a couple of days," she reminded him and herself although it felt longer. It felt as if she'd gone forever without seeing his face, without feeling his touch.

"I've been going out of my mind worrying about you," he admitted as his arms closed tight around her.

"You've had Ty following me."

"For your protection," he insisted, then added, "and for my sanity."

"So you don't hate me?"

"I could never hate you, Ariel." He sighed, his breath stirring her hair. "God, sometimes I wish I could. It would make it so much easier."

Goose bumps rose up on her skin at his ominous tone. "Make what so much easier, David?"

"To walk away."

"You don't want me anymore?" she asked, shifting her body closer to his so her breasts pressed against his chest.

He dragged in an audible breath. "I think I'm always going to want you…until the day I die." His hands cupped her face as his lips met hers.

At the touch of his mouth, passion whipped up inside her, banishing the last of her fears. Maybe she was the witch, but he was the one who'd cast the spell on her. She was completely under his power.

He lifted her, as he had that other night. But now there was no tenderness, no control, only raw desire and desperate need. As he walked toward the bedroom with her cradled in one arm, he pulled her clothes off with his free hand.

Buttons ricocheted like bullets around the hall as he tore her blouse from her shoulders. Then her gauzy Bohemian skirt followed, his fist rending the seam of the thin fabric. It fell in the doorway as he carried her into his room.

Instead of laying her on the bed, he set her on her feet. Her legs trembled beneath her, threatening to fold. "David…" She barely managed the protest before his mouth covered hers, his tongue thrusting between her parted lips.

His hands moved over her body, rough with passion, bruising in intensity as he cupped her breasts. His thumbs flicked ruthlessly back and forth across her nipples. He had never touched her like this, with anger and resentment simmering beneath the passion.

She had done this to him with her doubts and ac-cusations. She'd made him lose control. Instead of scaring her, though, he excited her, his hungry, des-perate need crumbling the last of her defenses.

A moan burned her throat, but she couldn't utter it. Her mouth was full, his tongue sliding in and out of her lips. Then one of his hands glided down her stomach, over the heat of her mound. A finger slipped inside her, then two, imitating the delicious friction of his tongue in her mouth.

She shuddered inside as an orgasm flowed through her and she dragged her mouth from his to moan. She'd barely caught her breath before he slid his fingers into her mouth. She tasted the sweetness of her own passion, and as she did, he watched her, his dark gaze hot and wild.

She suckled his fingers, pulling them deeper into her mouth, slipping her tongue between them. He shuddered now. "I have to have your mouth… on me…."

Naked, she dropped to her knees before him. Her fingers trembling, she dragged down the zipper on his jeans. Then she pushed them and his black silk boxers down. His penis jumped, long and hard, the veins throbbing in the engorged flesh. She closed her lips around it, flicking her tongue across the smooth, wet tip of it.

Her heart beat fast as excitement coursed through her. He'd never let her touch him like this before, had never made himself so vulnerable to her. But he didn't totally relinquish control. His hand fisted in her hair, pulling her mouth up and down his length. His ragged breaths echoed in the room until he stiffened against her and shouted just her name. "Ariel!"

She swallowed, then licked her lips. She would forever taste him. He would forever be a part of her now. "David, I love you," she murmured, rising up higher on her knees to wrap her arms around his waist.

But he pulled away. Without his warmth, goose bumps rose along her bare skin, and she shivered.

Was it over, just this? Could he not completely forgive her for doubting him? But even as she wondered, he dropped to his knees in front of her. Cupping her face, he kissed her, at first softly, tenderly, as he always had. But then the passion built again. He thrust his tongue between her lips before pulling his mouth away. His lips slid across her jaw, down the arch of her throat. His teeth nipped at her neck, then his tongue flicked across the bruised flesh.

"No one has ever done that to me," he told her, his mouth against her bare shoulder, his breath tickling her sensitive skin.

She knew why; it hadn't been so much an issue of control as of trust. She hadn't been the only one struggling with it.

His mouth moved lower, gliding over the curve of her breast, tracing it with the tip of his tongue. Then that tip flicked across a distended nipple.

She cried out as if he'd pinched her. Then he did, squeezing her other nipple between his thumb and forefinger while he suckled at this one, tugging with his teeth, then stroking with his tongue.

She arched her back, giving the control over to him as he played her body. Sensations rippled through her, heat and chills. Then ecstasy as another orgasm tore through her, convulsing between her legs.

He pushed her back on the hard floor and moved over her, jerking her knees over his shoulders as he placed his lips on the hottest, most sensitive part of her. She sobbed as another orgasm ripped through her. "David, oh, David!"

Tears trickled from beneath her closed lids, sliding down the sides of her face to dampen her tangled hair.

But he was relentless, dragging climax after climax from her body before he buried the length of his erection inside her. Nothing separated skin from skin as he drove in and out. Her muscles contracted, squeezing his thickness as she convulsed on an orgasm so great screams tore from her throat, echoing his guttural cries as he spilled inside her.

David rolled, pulling her limp body from the cold, hard floor to lay atop his sweat-slick chest. "Ariel...."

"What did we just do?" she asked. They hadn't used any protection.

"I don't know," he said, shuddering in the aftermath. "I've never lost it like that. I love you so much, Ariel…"

Tears burned her eyes, but she didn't fight them. She didn't fight her feelings for David anymore. "I love you, too."

More importantly, she trusted him, so she had to tell him everything. Returning to the church with her might put him in danger, but she wanted no more secrets between them. She rubbed her bare arms.

"You're cold," he murmured, lifting her to lay her in the bed. He pulled the covers over them both, folding her close against his side.

She wasn't just cold. She was scared. "David, I have to tell you something…."

He stiffened, perhaps bracing himself for another accusation.

"I found this church—"

"Ty mentioned it to me, that you were looking for Irina there. You think she's homeless?"

"Elena does."

"Elena also thinks I'm a killer. She's wrong about that, she's probably wrong about Irina, too."

Ariel nodded her agreement. Until Elena accepted her ability as a gift, she wouldn't be able to understand it. "Maybe. I didn't find Irina in the church, but I did find something."

His voice rumbled low and deep in his chest, against which her head lay. "What?"

Despite the warmth of his arms, she shivered again. "Someone had carved the symbols of the charms into the altar, David. The killer's been there."

"You don't know that—"

"I saw him. Not his face—he was wearing some kind of cloak like a monk's robes." Her breath shuddered out with remembered fear. "I didn't trip and fall like I told Ty. Someone hit me."

His hands shook as he lifted her face. No bumps and bruises remained from that day at the church, just a thin scratch where she'd caught the glancing blow. His fingertip traced it. "Ariel, you can't go back there."

"To find the killer, I have to, David. I want you to come with me."

His arms tightened around her. "Ty checked it out already. The area's full of vagrants. One of them probably hit you, intending to mug you." He squeezed her closer. "Or worse…"

"But the charms—"

He pressed his finger against her lips. "Shh…we'll figure it out, Ariel. We'll keep you safe."

She should have felt safe in his arms, held tight against his chest. But instead a chill of foreboding raced across her skin. She might not have her sister's ability to see the future, but she was intuitive enough to know that something bad was going to happen.

Or maybe it already had…

Ariel's eyes opened to darkness. She reached out, her hands sliding over the satin sheets. But she found no one else in the bed. She was alone. Again.

"David…"

Nobody responded, but the orange light glowed in the darkness, illuminating smoke and the image of her mother. The woman's mouth moved, her voice just a whisper. "Ariel…"

Ariel pressed her hands against her ears like a child afraid to hear a nightmare. She'd lived too many of those already. "No…go away," she pleaded, fear gripping her over what her mother might say.

Mama's image wavered in and out of focus, growing fainter and fainter.

Why was she really sending her mother away? Because she didn't want to hear what the woman had to say…about David? Because she didn't want to face the truth.

But deep down she didn't want her mother to leave. Memories swept through her, of the time in her childhood when she'd been happy, when she'd been with her family. She reached for the little pewter sun, clutching the charm between her fingers. As always, it was warm, and not just from the proximity with her skin. Even when she was cold, the sun never was. It always held warmth. And power.

The light extinguished and the darkness reigned again. With a trembling hand, Ariel reached for the lamp on the nightstand, bringing back a small circle of light. Then she pulled open the drawer where David had had his gun before. Like him, it was gone.

But her mother wasn't. She whispered her name. "Ariel…"

Ariel fumbled beside the bed for her clothes. "Mama?"

Orange light glowed under the bedroom door. Ariel pulled on her clothes, tying a knot in the tails to hold together her buttonless shirt. The voluminous folds of the skirt covered the tear in the fabric. Then she followed the light as if hypnotized. She opened the door and stepped out into the hall, into the thickness of smoke and the cloying fragrance of sandalwood and lavender.

"Ariel…" the voice beckoned from behind the door of David's den.

Ariel reached out a trembling hand, turning the knob until the door opened. She stepped over the threshold into darkness. No light from the hall or anywhere else shone into the room. Instead of reaching for a switch on the wall, she summoned a ghost. "Mama…"

The orange light flickered, low at first, like a candle about to burn out. Then it brightened enough to cast an eerie glow around the room, as if a fire burned within it. Dark paneling adorned the walls, its color echoed in the mahogany desk, file cabinets and bookshelves, every bit of it oozing masculinity, like David did. In every way, it was *his* room.

Ariel bowed her head, hesitant to invade a space that was so much David's inner sanctum. She knew how he valued his privacy. She stepped back, intending to leave, when her mother rose from the smoke. "Ariel…"

"What, Mama? What do you want me to see?" she asked.

The ghost drifted deeper into the room, pointing to a section of the dark paneling. "Look here, Ariel…"

As Ariel drew closer to the wall against which her mother stood, she noticed the handle, nearly indiscernible against the dark wood. When she pulled it, the paneling swung open on creaky hinges, revealing a secret closet.

Her heart raced as her breathing grew shallow, her lungs laboring for each breath. Inside the closet hung an ugly brown hooded robe and a rope. The thick braided fibers could have just been a belt… although it reminded her of a noose.

Alone that might have meant nothing to her, but there were photos and articles taped to the inside of the closet door, all about the fate befitting witches, how to conduct a witch hunt, how to rid the world of evil witchcraft.

"Oh, God, not David…"

She could taste him yet on her lips, feel him inside her…and all the while he'd intended to kill her? It couldn't be. He couldn't be the one who'd killed her mother, who'd burned her at the stake.

"No, Mama, tell me it wasn't…"

The orange glow intensified to a blinding light, as if an inferno now raged. "Ariel…"

"Was it David?" Ariel asked, her voice breaking with the effort to fight back her sobs. "Was it?"

"I can't say…."

"Why? Do I have to find out for myself? Is that it?" She bit back a threatening sob. "By then it might be too late." For her and her sisters.

Her mother's ghost pointed toward the robe. "He wore that, with the hood up."

The same garment Ariel had glimpsed on the man who'd attacked her at the church. "The church…"

"I've followed him there," her mother admitted.

"I don't know if he's just a member of the cult. Or the leader."

"The killer."

Elena's prophecy echoed in Ariel's head. *The man who's going to kill you—it's David Koster.*

Heart pounding wildly, Ariel climbed the crumbling steps to the graffiti-covered doors of the old church. Someone had removed the padlock and chains so the doors stood partially open. Light spilled from the building, casting eerie-colored patterns onto the surrounding warehouses through the broken stained-glass windows. Along with the disjointed peal of the swaying bell, chanting emanated from the church. *"Exstinguo…veneficus…"*

Ariel shuddered as she called on her college Latin to translate the words. *Extinguish witchcraft, kill the witches.* She should leave, go someplace safe and call the police. Instead she reached up, checking to make sure the hood of the brown robe covered her hair and most of her face, the rope, so like a noose, tied at her waist.

Maybe she was crazy to come here after Elena had warned her about the vision, about how she would die. But Ariel would be crazier if she left the church before she learned the truth. About David. About the killer. She had to save her family.

Before she could walk through the doors, though, the smoke rose, thick and impenetrable, the orange light glaring. Her mother's ghost stood between her and the entrance, between Ariel and danger. "I have to do this," she whispered. "Mama, I have to…."

For *her*. For her sisters.

Her mother's eyes wide with fear, she shook her head. "Ariel, no…"

Drawing a deep breath, Ariel stepped into the light and the smoke, passing through her mother to enter the church. Instead of the cold draft legend associated with ghosts, warmth filled Ariel, the warmth of her mother's spirit, of her love. Inside the church, her mother faded, slipping away with the smoke and light, disappearing before Ariel's tear-blurred gaze.

Summoning her courage, she walked up the aisle to slide into a pew behind the chanters. Rows were filled with people in those brown robes, their heads covered with hoods. No one noticed her entrance; they were focused on the front of the church, where a man stood before the altar leading them in the chant. She needed to get closer so she could identify him.

Pulse racing, she slipped toward the side aisle, intending to creep closer. But before she could leave the pew, someone caught her wrist, embedding the charm into her skin. She couldn't lift the can of pepper spray—her one weapon—grasped in that hand.

"What the hell are you doing here?" a voice rasped, barely audible beneath the chanting. "Trying to get yourself killed?"

"Ty." His name spilled from her lips with a relieved breath. While she recognized his voice, his face remained in shadows beneath the hood.

"Let's get you out of here," he murmured, pushing her out of the pew, then passing her in the side aisle to lead the way to the back.

She drew up short against him as he stopped. Then she followed his gaze to the doors that someone had closed. Two people in robes stood before them as if guarding the exit.

"There's another way out," Ty whispered, his fingers tight around her wrist as he guided her farther down the side aisle.

Beneath the hood, hairs lifted at the nape of Ariel's neck. "How do you know?"

"That day I found you here, I came back. I checked the place out. That's when I got this robe. There's a pile of them in the vestibule."

"And tonight, did you follow me here?" When he shook his head, her heart jumped. "You followed David."

"You told me to," he reminded her, his voice soft. He found a door off the aisle, opening it to darkness. "This is a stairwell to the basement," he whispered close to her ear. "It's old and not very secure, but it's safer than staying up here with these lunatics."

Before seeing if she agreed, he plunged into the darkness. Ariel trembled, hating the fear weakening her knees, numbing her mind. She needed the light. She needed the warm comfort of it and the smoke. *Mama...*

Where was she?

"Ariel..." But it was Ty's voice calling her as he tightened his fingers around her wrist and pulled her down the first couple of steps.

Ariel stumbled, the stairs creaking beneath her weight. "Where's David?" she asked, glancing over her shoulder toward the altar. But the man, the leader of this odd cult, was gone.

Ty pulled the door shut behind them, then switched on a flashlight, the small beam bouncing off cobwebs and rotted boards. "I don't know. Once he got inside the church, I lost him."

"We have to find him, Ty," she said, her voice quavering as the doubts assailed her. "I have to know if he's..."

"He's not," his friend insisted.

Something about his tone sent a chill racing

across Ariel's skin. How was Ty so certain that David wasn't the killer? Because *he* was?

A scream burned the back of her throat, threatening to escape. She bit back the need to run, afraid of alerting the chanters. They couldn't find out who she was. *Kill the witches.*

"Where's the other way out?" she asked, trying to hide the suspicion churning in her stomach and messing with her head. "This is a basement."

"It's got an outside door," he told her.

Doubt slowed her steps as he tried tugging her down the steep steps. Dare she trust him? The beam of his flashlight illuminated only a small circle, boards that had fallen through the church floor into the basement atop old crates and other debris.

She tried wriggling from his grasp. "I need to hold on to the railing," she insisted as the steps creaked beneath her.

"I've got you."

That was what she feared. "Ty, let me go," she beseeched him, tugging at her wrist. "You don't want to do this. You don't want to hurt me."

"Ariel!" His grip tightened as she struggled with him. "I'm not going to hurt you. I have to get you to safety." As he said it, the stairwell groaned beneath their weight, boards cracking and splintering.

The steps giving way beneath his feet, Ty

released her and clutched at the railing. But that old, rotted wood broke, too. Off balance, he fell back. Ariel reached for him, catching the coarse fabric of his robe between her fingers. "Ty!"

He was too heavy; she wasn't strong enough. The fabric slipped from her grasp. Arms flailing, Ty fell into the darkness. His flashlight, torn from his grasp, flew, its beam bouncing around the basement like a strobe light before striking and breaking apart on the cement floor.

The way Ty's body might have. Heart hammering with fear and regret, Ariel scrambled over the broken steps, clawing at the rotted, breaking wood so she wouldn't fall through herself. "Ty! Oh, my God, Ty!"

Praying for her mother's guidance, Ariel fumbled around in the darkness, banging into those wooden crates, tripping over boards as she tried to find Ty.

"Mama!" she cried, tears streaking through the grime covering her face. "Help me!"

Her feet struck something softer than wood, and she stumbled, falling onto a body.

"Ty, thank God!" Her hands ran over him, feeling for a heartbeat. His chest rose and fell weakly, his breathing shallow. Suddenly a light appeared, not the orange glow or the faint glimmer. She turned toward it, blinded by the brightness, unable to make out more than a shadow of the man standing behind it.

"Help me," she implored him. "He's alive, but he's hurt."

"Use your witchcraft to heal him," the man said, his voice deep with bitterness.

She swallowed down her fear, bluffing. "I'm not a witch."

The man helped her to her feet, yanking her up by her hair. The hood had fallen off as she'd struggled to find Ty. "You're a liar, like your mother. You're not getting away from me again."

"Why are you doing this?" Ariel asked, tears of pain streaming from her eyes as she tried to pull her hair from his punishing grip. She jerked around, kicking out at his shins, but he pulled harder, tearing the hair at her temples.

"You're a witch," he insisted. "And all the witches must die."

"Why?" she wailed the question.

"To avenge my ancestors. To honor my family."

Despite his tight grasp, she shook her head. "No…it's more than that. You're the one lying now."

For a moment his grip loosened, and Ariel jerked free. Then something wrapped tight around her throat, coarse fibers biting into her skin. She choked, gagging on fear.

He laughed at her. "It's about power, too. Soon your power will be mine…."

Ariel gasped for breath, her fingers clawing at her throat to loosen the rope. "No…"

She didn't want to die like this, the way her sister had seen her, strung up like a witch.

Chapter 14

Her mother's words echoed in Ariel's head. *The charm will protect you.* Fighting her instincts to claw at the rope, she reached for her charm, closing her trembling fingers over the pewter sun.

The light poured in and with it rolled the smoke and mist. "Mama," Ariel whispered as she glanced up to where the light shone brightest, at the top of the stairs.

But the shadow standing there was tall and broad-shouldered and much more substantial than a ghost. David. He rushed down the steps, nearly slipping into the hole left by Ty. He struggled for his balance, grasping what was left of the rickety railing.

"Don't come any closer," the man warned him.

The rope tightened even more around Ariel's throat. Her vision dimmed as this world started slipping away from her. But she fought, focusing on the charm and David. He regained his balance quickly with an innate grace so much at odds with his size, but he stayed just a few steps below the hole, looking even bigger and more intimidating because he wasn't at their level.

"Stay back!" the man shouted, shaking with rage. "I'll kill her!"

"Then I'll kill you," David vowed, his deep voice vibrating with the threat as he pulled a gun from the pocket of the robe he wore. "Slowly. Painfully. I'll make you suffer."

"You're supposed to be one of my disciples. You're supposed to be loyal to *me!*" he screamed.

"I love *her*. I only came to the meetings to find you and stop you, so I could protect her. Hurt her and *you* die," David promised in that deep voice of authority that brooked no arguments.

Even as she gasped for breath, love warmed her. David hadn't betrayed her. He'd been doing everything in his power to protect her, even putting himself at risk. If only she'd trusted him and his love…

"Let her go!" David shouted.

Perhaps as a reflex to the authoritative tone, the

man loosened the rope, giving Ariel enough slack to pull it from his fingers. She dropped to her knees with the noose around her neck.

Before David could aim the gun, the man hurled a board at him, striking his arm. The gun clattered to the floor. But David wasn't about to let him get away. He launched himself off the stairs, knocking the man to the floor. They rolled across the cement, a tangle of fists and feet, throwing punches and kicks. David's breath hissed out, and a knife blade flashed, red with his blood.

Someone called Ariel's name softly, calling her back to the world of the living. "Ariel!" It was uttered now with more impatience. Her mother's voice, irritated that she couldn't hear.

"I hear you, Mama," she whispered, but now she was the one to bring no sound to her words, the rope having stolen her voice.

The eerie orange light brightened, shining on David's gun lying at the bottom of the stairs. Hands shaking, Ariel grabbed it, then trusted the light and her mother's voice to guide her to shoot the right man as she pulled the trigger.

One of the robed figures lurched to his feet, then scrambled over the crates and boards to the back of the basement. A door opened, light from the street spilling inside as men fled from the church. Horror gripped her. She'd shot the wrong man. Dropping the gun, she staggered to where he lay sprawled on the floor.

"David!" Although she screamed, his name was but a croak from her throat. Tears streamed down her face as she reached for him, running her hands down his arms. Her palms came away wet and sticky with his blood. "David! David, are you all right?" *Oh, please, God!*

His dark eyes blinked open, staring up at her. One hand came up to cup her face, while his other tugged at the noose, pulling it loose from her throat.

She nodded. "David, you're bleeding…" Tears choked her voice. "Oh, God. I shot you."

He tipped her chin so her gaze met his eyes. "No, you shot him. But his knife nicked me. It's nothing…"

From the blood seeping like a rich merlot into the cement floor, she doubted it. "David…"

"Ariel, I didn't want you knowing about this place, about the cult. I wanted to keep you safe."

"You did," she assured him. "It was my fault. You got hurt because of me. We have to get you out of here," she said, her fear returning. She bit her lip, remembering who else had been hurt because of her. "And Ty."

"What about Ty?" David asked, then with slight panic shouted his best friend's name. "Ty!"

"I'm here," Ty called back, his voice a guttural groan. "I'm alive."

Not all right. Just alive.

She had to get help. Drawing in a deep breath, she stood and turned for the stairs. "I'll be right back," she promised them, but someone in a dark robe stood at the top of the stairs, blocking her escape.

Were they all there? All the chanters? She crouched down, feeling around the cement floor for the gun. If she had to shoot them all, she would. For David.

"You don't need that," her mother's voice promised her. As the ghost spoke, the person on the stairs lowered her hood, the orange glow shimmering in her blond hair.

She didn't ask how her sister had found her. She'd obviously had another dream, and now, because of Ariel's questions, she'd paid attention to the details. And she'd found her.

"I called the police," Elena said. Sirens wailed in the distance, growing louder as they approached. "Help's coming."

Help had already arrived. In the form of Ariel's mother's ghost and her sister. All Ariel had had to do was trust—in her gift, in the people she cared about and in herself.

* * *

"Are you all right? Do you have everything you need?" Ariel asked as she sat on the edge of the bed near David. He'd insisted on coming home, and as always, he had gotten his way, the emergency room doctors releasing him despite their reservations.

"No, I don't," David said, leaning back against the satin sheets with a pitiful sigh.

"Do you need another painkiller?" Ariel asked, reaching for the prescription bottle on the nightstand. The seal across the top had yet to be broken. "You haven't taken any."

"I don't need them."

"What do you need?" she asked with a smile as the hand on his uninjured arm reached for her, sliding up and down her thigh.

"You, Ariel. All I need is you." He leaned forward, kissing her lips.

"David," she said, "you have to be careful so you don't aggravate your wound."

"It's really not that bad, Ariel."

"His knife nicked an artery. You lost a lot of blood," she reminded him.

"I'm fine." He sighed, leaning back on the mound of pillows propped against the black leather headboard. "I'm better than Ty."

"He's going to be okay," she insisted. "He was lucky. A broken leg, a sprained wrist, a concussion." She catalogued his injuries. "He'll fully recover."

Physically. She wasn't so sure about mentally or emotionally. When Ariel had visited his hospital room before taking David home, she'd found Haylee beside his bed. The little girl understood him; she wouldn't leave him alone. Guilt nagged at Ariel. Ty had feelings for her, feelings she wished he didn't have, feelings she couldn't return. Her heart belonged to David.

"He'll be okay," David agreed, obviously speaking of more than his injuries. Since they had been friends for so long, he had to have known about his friend's interest in her.

"Will *we* be okay?" Ariel asked, hastening to add, "I don't mean *us*. I mean my sisters, my family." The witches.

"Oh, God, Ariel," he groaned, "you still don't think that I'm—"

She leaned forward and pressed her fingers against his lips. "No. I don't. And I didn't." But for a short, horrible time. "I know now you were trying to catch the killer."

She should have realized that he hadn't just been looking for her sisters. David's nature wouldn't have allowed him to ignore the threat against her life. Just as he'd protected Ty all those years ago, he had always intended to protect her.

"You should have told me," she insisted, "especially when I asked you about the church. I could have helped." Instead of feeling helpless.

He shook his head. "That's why I kept it secret about the cult. I'd found them on the Internet, talking about witchcraft and witches. It fit with what you'd told me about the vendetta, about the witch hunt."

"So you did believe me?"

"Always. But I knew you'd want to get involved, and I couldn't risk losing you. I couldn't risk something going wrong."

As it had, because of her lack of trust. "How long did you know about the cult?" she asked.

He shrugged, then winced as the bandage pulled at the wound on his arm. "Ever since our first trip to Armaya, I'd been searching for individuals or groups who might be crazy enough to start a witch hunt."

While she'd started searching for her sisters, he'd been looking for the killer all along. "So who is he?" she asked.

David shook his head. "Despite all my digging and my pretense of wanting to join the cult, I couldn't fool this guy into revealing his identity. I don't know who he is. I couldn't even trace his e-mails, but I traced the others. None of them know his identity, though, and I don't think they had anything to do with the murders either." Frustration creased his forehead and narrowed his dark eyes. "But you're not going to be safe until we find *him,* Ariel."

She shook her head as she crawled into the bed beside him. "No, you're wrong," she argued as she rested her head on his chest. "I'm safe. Right here in your arms. How'd you know I was there tonight, in the basement?"

"You called me," David said, his forehead puckered as he remembered. "I heard you call my name."

Ariel shook her head, brushing her hair across his chest. "I didn't...."

"You called my name, then I saw the light from the stairwell." He groaned before adding, "The orange light. Looked like the fires of hell were burning down here."

He'd seen it, too, and heard her mother. "David, that wasn't hell..."

He sighed. "That's where I'd be if I lost you." His arms tightened around her. "Ariel, I love you. I'd die before I'd let anyone hurt you." And he almost had.

"I know," she said, hoping he believed her. Knowing, as a grin spread across his face, that he did. "I love you, too, so much."

"Then show me," he challenged her with a wicked grin.

"You're hurt," she reminded him.

"So be gentle with me."

"David—"

His lips silenced her admonishment as they closed over hers in a deep kiss. His fingers, surprisingly nimble despite his wound, plucked at the knot tying her shirt closed.

She pulled back. "David, I can't believe what you did for me, how you put yourself at risk, joining that cult."

"I love you," he said simply, as if that explained his willingness to die for her.

Finally she understood real love and total acceptance. She would never doubt him again. "I'd do anything for you, too, David," she promised.

His wicked grin stole over his mouth. "Then make love to me."

She kissed him, first gently, just softly pressing her lips to his. Then she deepened the kiss, sliding her tongue into his mouth, enticing and teasing him until he groaned.

Out of concern, she stiffened and drew back. "Your arm?"

"What arm?" he scoffed.

"You're not hurting?" she asked, eyes narrowed as she studied his handsome face for any flicker of pain.

"Just with wanting you. I need you, Ariel." Then he grimaced as he added, "But…"

He was hurting.

"What?" she asked.

"You're going to have to do all the work."

A smile teased across her lips as she intended to tease him. The heady rush of power triggered the rapid rate of her pulse, heating her blood and fueling her passion. She shrugged his good arm off her shoulders and stood up.

"Ariel…"

"I'm not going anywhere," she promised him as she slowly slid the straps of her black satin bra down her arms. Then she undid the clasp between her breasts, letting it fall away.

David groaned. But she knew his physical hurt had nothing to do with his injury. He shifted against the bed and reached for her.

Ariel stepped back, out of the circle of his arms. Turning around, she presented him with her bare back as she shimmied out of her torn skirt. She wiggled her hips once, twice, until the gauzy fabric slowly slid down over her hips and legs, pooling at her feet. She took her time with her panties, hooking a finger in the lace at her hip. With a peek over her shoulder at David's face, his dark eyes hot as he

raptly studied her, she slowly pulled the satin down
the length of her legs.

"Ariel, you're ki—you're—"

David, speechless—that was an unusual state for
him. But then, so was this—her in control and him
the one on the bed helpless with desire. His face
flushed, a muscle ticking in his cheek. "Damn it,
come here," he growled at her.

She turned to face him and shook her head, her
silky hair sliding back and forth across her breasts
in an inadvertent caress. She bit her lip, then
reached up and cupped her breasts, as if holding
them up for his inspection.

He kicked back the sheet as if to stand, but she
pushed him down, her hands firm on his shoulders.
"Not so fast," she warned him. But he caught her
around the waist with one arm, lifting her enough
that he was able to close his lips around a nipple.

Ariel moaned as passion spread from her
breast to pool between her legs. She reached for
him, her hand gliding over his silk boxers to the
hard ridge of his erection. As he'd once tortured
her with the sheets, she slid her hand up and
down, using the silk for delicious friction as she
pumped him.

"Ariel." He groaned. "I want you! *Now!*"

Even weakened by blood loss, the man was

commanding. Powerful. Ariel pushed his boxers down, then she mounted him, taking him deep within her, closing her muscles around him as she'd closed her hand.

She bit her lip as her passion ignited even more, burning hotly inside her. She rocked her hips, then rode him up and down. He held one hip, helping her frenzied pace. Then he lifted up and bent his neck forward until his mouth closed around her nipple again, tugging at one, then the other, pulling orgasms from her body as she shuddered against him.

He stiffened and shouted out her name. "Ariel! I love you!"

Ariel laid her head against David's chest, damp with perspiration. God, the man was passionate. No matter how long they had together, she'd never tire of him, never want him any less than she did now. And she'd only love him more. She turned the diamond on her finger.

"I've made up my mind," she told him.

"About what?" he asked, his chest moving up and down as he struggled to regain his breath.

"Your question," she reminded him. "I have an answer for you if you still want one."

He closed his eyes as if overcome with emotion. "I want one. I want *you*. Forever."

"So let's set a date," she said.

"Really?" he asked, his eyes bright with hope.

"Oh, so you just gave me the ring to shut me up," she teased as she snuggled against his chest. "To stop me from nagging you for a commitment."

He laughed, his chest rising and falling beneath her cheek. "Yeah, you're such a nag."

"You were warned," she said with no sympathy. "That's why I want to set a date—so you don't change your mind and back out."

"Never." He reached across her, grimacing as the bandage on his arm moved. "Hand me the phone."

"For what?"

"I'm going to speed-dial a judge, get him over here to marry us pronto."

"You're not getting out of it that cheap," she said, clicking her tongue in mock disgust. "I want a wedding. A big one. And I want all my family there."

David sighed. "Ariel, I want to promise you that you'll have that. But…"

She pressed her fingers against his lips again. "Shh…you don't have to promise me any-thing…but to love me forever."

He grinned. "Done."

"So let's set a date."

He nodded even though skepticism darkened his eyes. "You decide. I'll be there."

"You better be," she threatened, her heart lurching at the thought that he almost hadn't been—if the knife had cut a little deeper, if she'd shot the wrong man. But her mother had guided her and the charm had made her strong. Trusting them, trusting herself, had been the right thing to do.

"I wouldn't miss the first day of the rest of our lives for anything," he promised.

She settled back in his arms, content. "This is the first day," she said. "The wedding is just the party to share the commitment with our friends and family."

"I am committed to you, Ariel," he vowed. "To our love. To the life we'll build together."

Ariel nodded. "Me, too."

And they would have a life. She was sure of it. She felt safe, not just in David's arms but with the orange glow shining under the bedroom door.

She realized now that her mother had been watching over her for her whole life. As she'd brought David to Ariel's rescue, she would keep them safe.

For the first time in her life, Ariel had no doubts—about David and his love, about who and what she was…or about the future they would build together.

She trusted that she would be reunited with both her sisters and that the killer would be caught before he killed again.

Epilogue

With shaking hands, he gripped the pewter trifold frame. Through eyes blurred with pain and rage, he stared at the redheaded girl in the middle. She had been the easiest to find but the hardest to kill. She was stronger than she looked and far more powerful.

His head throbbed, the pain hammering at his temples in rhythm with his rapid heartbeat. He'd been so close. He'd had the noose wrapped tight around her throat. She'd nearly breathed her last. But for *him,* the man trapped under her spell, so bewitched that he would lay down his life for hers. God, she was a witch!

His shoulder throbbed, burning with pain from the bullet she'd put in him. He had connections, though, knew a doctor who asked no questions. The bullet wound wouldn't kill him, but she might. He had to be stronger before he took her on again. For now, he'd leave her alone.

He dropped the frame on his desk, fumbled open the bottom drawer and reached for his flask. After twisting off the cap, he sucked down a fiery swallow.

He'd wait to kill her...after he'd killed her sisters. Then she'd be weaker. And he would be stronger. He needed their combined powers to do what modern medicine could not—to stop the inoperable tumor growing inside his head. Before it killed him.

He leaned back in his chair and closed his eyes. In his head, the witches danced. The hoods of their robes covering their faces and all but the bright red of their smiling mouths, they moved in and out of the flames that threatened to consume him.

But that wouldn't happen. He would kill them first. Fighting against the pain, he opened one eye and glanced down at the picture frame. His gaze fell upon the blond girl. He'd seen the very same face, framed by pale hair, just recently. The daughter looked exactly as her mother had twenty years ago. But no one would ever know if she would continue to look like her as she aged because the child would grow no older.

She would die. Soon.

* * * * *

Look for Elena's story, Persecuted,
the next book in the WITCH HUNT *series,
coming September 2008 only from
Mills & Boon® Intrigue.*

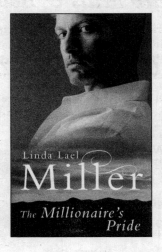

Celebrate 100 years of pure reading pleasure with Mills & Boon®

To mark our centenary, each month we're publishing a special 100th Birthday Edition. These celebratory editions are packed with extra features and include a FREE bonus story.

Plus, you have the chance to enter a fabulous monthly prize draw. See 100th Birthday Edition books for details.

Now that's worth celebrating!

July 2008

The Man Who Had Everything by Christine Rimmer
Includes FREE bonus story *Marrying Molly*

August 2008

Their Miracle Baby by Caroline Anderson
Includes FREE bonus story *Making Memories*

September 2008

Crazy About Her Spanish Boss by Rebecca Winters
Includes FREE bonus story
Rafael's Convenient Proposal

Look for Mills & Boon® 100th Birthday Editions at your favourite bookseller or visit
www.millsandboon.co.uk

FREE

4 BOOKS AND A SURPRISE GIFT!

We would like to take this opportunity to thank you for reading this Mills & Boon® book by offering you the chance to take FOUR more specially selected titles from the Intrigue series absolutely FREE! We're also making this offer to introduce you to the benefits of the Mills & Boon® Book Club™—

- ★ **FREE home delivery**
- ★ **FREE gifts and competitions**
- ★ **FREE monthly Newsletter**
- ★ **Books available before they're in the shops**
- ★ **Exclusive Mills & Boon Book Club offers**

Accepting these FREE books and gift places you under no obligation to buy; you may cancel at any time, even after receiving your free shipment. Simply complete your details below and return the entire page to the address below. You don't even need a stamp!

YES! Please send me 4 free Intrigue books and a surprise gift. I understand that unless you hear from me, I will receive 6 superb new titles every month for just £3.15 each, postage and packing free. I am under no obligation to purchase any books and may cancel my subscription at any time. The free books and gift will be mine to keep in any case.

I8ZEE

Ms/Mrs/Miss/Mr...Initials ....

BLOCK CAPITALS PLEASE

Surname ....

Address ....

....

....Postcode ....

Send this whole page to:
The Mills & Boon Book Club, FREEPOST CN81, Croydon, CR9 3WZ